MORNINGSTAR
PRESS

SCHISM,

Something Is Amiss In Heaven Again!

ALSO BY ARMANDO MINUTOLI

FICTION

THE HESTER STREET KIDS

A Drama/Thriller, which provides an historical view of the power of Sicilian Mob in 1950's New York.

NON-FICTION

MEDJUGORJE, A PILGRIM'S JOURNEY

Apparitions of the Blessed Virgin Mary in Bosnia-Hercovinia

SCREENPLAYS

Mr. Minutoli is also the author of two screenplay adaptations

THE HESTER STREET KIDS and SCHISM

SCHISM

Something Is Amiss In Heaven Again!

Armando Minutoli

The Morning Star Press
DELRAY BEACH, FLORIDA

Armando Minutoli/The Morning Star Press
Delray Beach, Florida
www.themorningstarpress.com. Email: aminutoli@earthlink.net

Publisher's Note: This is a work of fiction. Names, characters, places, and incidents are a product of the author's imagination. Locales and public names are sometimes used for atmospheric purposes. Any resemblance to actual people, living or dead, or to businesses, companies, events, institutions, or locales is completely coincidental.

Book Layout & Design ©2015 – Armando and Consuelo Minutoli
Bookcover artwork designed by C.G.I. Artist Mike "Mr.Mike", Herzog

SCHISM, Something Is Amiss In Heaven Again!
/Armando Minutoli. -- 1st ed.
ISBN 978-096-3054487
ISBN-13: 978-1518812415
ISBN-10: 1518812414:
Library of Congress Catalog Card No: 2015910186

For
My Long Lost Eldest Sister Liliana Minutoli and My Nieces, Loredana and Barbara Lombardi and Family in Genoa, Italy.

"In my Father's House, there are many mansions"
[Jn. 14:2]

PART ONE

One

THE SKY SHOWED GRAY. A cold wind blew, swirling and lifting leaves onto the town rail platform, a bland construct devoid of artistic design and painted in municipal gray. Its lamps flickered as they haphazardly extinguished, in expectation of the light of the new day.

The pallid backdrop mirrored Tony Romero's dilemma as he stood bracing his Brooks Brothers-suited body on a Hartsdale signpost. His weary frame conveyed a picture of the past night's exploits; either that of a corporate warrior, or one now stained with disgrace.

Once confident, today he felt conspicuous in the assembling crowd of commuters who, like him, awaited the southbound express. He shivered; the pre-winter chill paralleled the sense of doom he felt within--as one on the precipice of meeting the gallows.

Dejected, he lamented in a labored whisper, "I lost her... I lost everything... Maybe God too."

Two

THE LOBBY OF NINETY-NINE WALL bustled as securities analysts and stock traders made their way to their offices above. The height of their floor was a measure of success for them, and they took pride in allowing others to see which floor buttons they pushed.

They shared an adrenalin-induced energy, readied for explosion, in pursuit of making the financial killing of the day.

Tony Romero, of their breed, pushed his way through the rotating entrance doors and was greeted by his waiting partner, Albee Donna, a tall burly man with a pronounced Roman nose that formed an anatomical in-line with his protruding mid-section.

"Hey, Tony, wow! We had some night last night... sometin hah... those broads didn't want to quit," he recalled with bravado, tightening his silk tie.

"Don't remind me, Albee. My back is killing me and Norma is pissed big time."

Albee noticed Tony's limited response, but not the panic on his face. Tony did not want to accept that his marriage was on the line. Albee assumed that his partner was suffering a bout of guilt, and offered a pompous defense for their actions.

"Yeah, but they can't complain too much, we give 'em everything."

Tony, in an effort to avoid further discussion, stopped to alter his course and escape the conversation. "Albee, wait. You go up. I forgot to get the papers," he said, and without waiting for a reply made for the corner newsstand.

The crowded booth trailed a line of people. Tony slowed and noticed a little girl, of pre-school age, absorbed in hopscotch on and off the curb, unaware of a truck backing in.

A nearby doorman showed off his self-importance by dusting his bright red military-like uniform and barking instructions, which caused a distraction for the driver of the two-and-a-half-tonner. The husky, unshaven man flipped up his undersized cap with fury and stretched his bulging neck out the window to deliver a flurry of defiant expletives.

While the verbal battle ensued, his truck rolled. Their heated comebacks left them both blind and deaf to shouts of warning.

The child's parents were equally otherwise absorbed as they rummaged through the daily papers, in an obsessive search for their theater reviews.

A catastrophe was about to happen.

Tony yelled and made a saving dash for the child. In doing so, he lost his footing, yet was still able to whisk her from harm's way. He, however, was not so lucky. His urgent motion caused his head to meet the truck's back bumper with an audible thud, and he fell atop the child, comatose, his blood staining his starched collared shirt.

Alerted by the louder screams of pedestrians, the child's parents wrenched their heads around to see their daughter lying unresponsive beneath his motionless body, and rushed to her in a panic.

Three

Earlier That Morning

NORMA ROMERO HAD BECOME despondent, on the verge of throwing her cards in. Empty now, with vengeance on her mind, she waited on the dark side of dawn.

In a daze, she went through the motions of a proverbial homemaker, anchored at the kitchen sink, the helm of her lush Westchester colonial. Her back ached as it supported her shapely five-foot frame, pinched from a restless night's sleep of protest on the studio couch.

She prepared today, not to lay a course for household activity, but to seek justice. No, this day was different; she had a clear target. She pounded her fist on the kitchen counter as his image invaded her mind's eye. She flew at him, and then at God, asking inside, *Why did You let this happen?*

More than anything, Norma wanted to turn the clock back, but reality took hold. Conscious now that the life she had lived was one haunted by secrets and mistrust, she internalized her fury.

What a fool I've been, she admonished herself. Her mind reeled through the playbacks of the many nights she had lain naked in their marital bed, wanting him, trying to compete with unseen ghosts for his affection. Those unseen ghosts had infiltrated their sacred vows.

Soon the sound of tapping shoes broke the morning quiet, alerting her to his descent, which elevated her contempt. She made the sign of the cross, as if in defense of an impending evil; or maybe, she realized more so to control the feeling of violence that bubbled inside her.

"Hey, where are the kids?" he asked in his morning voice, once sweet to her ears.

She choked out a reply, "At... my mother's." Then she flailed her tightened fist into the air. "If you were home at night, you would know where they were, wouldn't you?" she accused.

It was the eve of their anniversary, and, for Norma, a failed milestone realized. She wailed inside as her prized green eyes fixed cold in disdain. "Ten wasted years," she mouthed in a whisper, with tightening muscles seeming to increase her opulent frame.

"What are you doing all dressed up? No coffee?" he asked casually, buttoning his suit jacket, ignoring her words.

Fuming, she fired back, "I'm afraid you'll have to make it for yourself this morning; in fact, from now on."

A crashing sound of a plate accompanied her words.

"You're out of control!" he shouted, bracing his head, throbbing from a hangover. "What is your problem?" he added with impatience.

Her ponytail cut into the tense air as she spun at him again, eyes full of venom. "*I'm* out of control, Tony? No. No," she repeated. Her ample chest heaved, and she gave him the middle finger.

"No!" she asserted once more, in a screech deep from her gut. "*You're* out of control. *You're* the problem!" she declared, pounding the air once again. "I'm tired of washing lipstick off your shirts and ignoring the so-called rashes on your neck! I deserve better, you - you bum!"

Tony threw her a dazed look, like that of a bird held in a cat's jaw, and sputtered a weak reply. "You don't know what you're talking about. You're not going anywhere," he said with a palm-up wave of his hand. He made light of Norma's accusations by picking through the mail on the counter.

This tactic only added to her fury, evidenced by the sound of another breaking dish. The shattering sound resonated through the stillness of the plush kitchen.

"The soles of your fancy Italian shoes won't hold up under the heat, where you're going."

Overwhelmed with emotion, her thoughts swung to self-doubt: *Have I failed him? Was I the foolish one, living in a fantasy, still in awe of him like on the night of our prom: my handsome Prince, my lover?* She lamented silently, under a cascade of tears.

Her heart filled with more grief as her mind flashed snapshots that recalled the hope she once had. *It was not to be this way,* she protested inside herself. *We were to be forever, soulmates.* Grief overtook her anger, until the sound of his voice interrupted her thoughts.

"I don't know what you're talking about."

Her face flushed red, and her feelings of anguish changed to those of hate. She was suddenly poised for sharp retaliation.

Tony nervously shook out a goodbye, "Gotta go, I'm late for the train. I guess I'll have breakfast in the city." He had betrayed her, and he knew it. The guilt he now felt for her pain cut deep into him; he had destroyed her world, her innocence, and her dreams. He knew their lives were never to be the same.

"Yeah, why don't you? Hopefully you'll choke on it."

"Hey, stop now, we'll talk about this nonsense tonight," he pleaded, in a stumbled delay of the inevitable; his words were littered with false indignation, punctuated by an escaping foot out the back door. His exit, though, was not fast enough to shield the blow of a parting castigation.

"What a nice Catholic man, Tony." Her face screwed up in a grimace of fury. "You are a fake. You're going to hell, Romero," she fired at him. She flung another dish, this time at his heels, trailing his escape.

Four

IT SEEMED LIKE AN ETERNITY before the responding ambulance and police car signaled their arrival, their sirens blasting in demand of street space. Without hesitation, and with equipment in hand, the emergency crew burst from the ambulance to dispense assistance to both victims, the child being their priority. They quickly hoisted the injured on to gurneys and rolled them through the tail of the vehicle. Once settled, they urgently checked for vital signs as they administered oxygen and installed intravenous drips.

The injured were oblivious to the rock and tumble of the transport as it sped with urgent purpose. The driver's head dripped with sweat as his hands held tight to the wheel. He drove with skill, negotiating through a throng of pedestrians, vehicles and potholes in the maze of the city's morning traffic. Within desperate minutes, the truck backed in to a nearby hospital emergency.

A waiting team of doctors received them with worried looks as they accepted the unresponsive bodies into their care. The medical personnel were unaware that they had become witnesses to the fate of two souls who had unwittingly entwined their destinies.

The little girl's parents followed a police officer into a nearby waiting room. Propelled by frenetic energy, their faces mirrored fear and anguish--expressions that dimmed the oddity of their offbeat form of dress.

The worried parents spent an hour in futile pacing, until a large, round-faced nurse in a white starched uniform appeared. She brushed back her gray hair with the back of her hand and gave them a smile. The couple took this expression as a beacon of hope and rose to greet her.

"Come," she beckoned, with an expansive breath that lifted her robust chest. She latched on to the mother's hand.

"She's conscious and calling for Mom. Only has a minor contusion," the nurse said in a calm assuring tone. "Doctor is treating her for mild shock."

The mother sighed with relief, her legs so weak that lost her balance. Her husband, barely sure-footed himself, braced her up. The nurse patted them with understanding, and led them down the hall. Her voice was a mix of awe and admiration.

"Thank God. I understood it could have been much worse."

"Yes," agreed the mother. "If it were not for the man's quick action in shielding her body..."

"Oh my yes," the grateful father agreed as he tried to keep pace. Then he touched his chin, an inquisitive look on his face, and asked about the condition of the man who had saved his daughter. His words though, hung unanswered.

In a brief moment, they arrived at their daughter's dimly-lit room and rushed to her bedside. They found her resting peacefully with the help of a sedative. The doctor at her side happily nodded a greeting. He opened his mouth to share his diagnosis, but the girl's father interrupted him by questioning the nurse again. "How is the man?" This time his tone indicated that he insisted upon an answer.

The doctor signaled a rescue to the nurse with an "I got it" tap of his lab coat. She nodded gratefully, and he responded for her.

"Unfortunately, we don't know. He remains in a suspended state."

"Well, will he make it?" the father dug, guilt and remorse nagging inside him.

Reading his painful expression, the doctor replied with empathy, "All I can say is that his vital signs are not very good right now. However, there is always hope. I have seen rebounds with injuries of this kind. We pray this will be the case here."

Five

TONY WOKE WITH A JOLT. Disoriented, he tried to discern the strange surroundings. He barely felt the slowing beat of his heart as the room filled with sounds of static babble. Frantic voices shouted instructions over and around him.

"He's going... another 100 cc's... Paddles...again... Stand clear... again..." and then silence, until broken by the dreaded words: "He's gone... give me the time."

At that instant, Tony found himself without pain, cradled in a cushioned calm, which brought with it a euphoric sensation and a familiar tranquility.

Fully cognizant but slow to realize, he floated above the room with no inkling that he was the injured person lying below. Monitors and medical apparatuses whose lights blinked and expelled irritating noises obscured his sight.

In an instant, he realized where he was. *How did I get up here?* He thought to himself, and focused upon the body below that the doctors and nurses were working on. Curious, he repositioned himself to take a closer look, and was shocked by what he saw. *That's me!* he shouted. He was unable to grasp in full that he had separated from his body.

I must be dreaming, he said, bewildered and confused. He was further puzzled when he overheard the nurse speak sad words of closure.

"What a shame, Anthony. So young and handsome." She sighed as she smoothed his hair, then said to another nurse, "Let's disconnect and clean him up before his family gets here."

Fearful, Tony barked at them, *What the hell is going on? What is this?* He received no response and tried again.

Hey, are you deaf? I'm right up here!

His thoughts were distracted as he became aware of voices and sobs coming from the other side of the curtain. He instantly found himself floating above the little girl he had tried to rescue. She was now held safe in the arms of her parents, who were in the process of thanking her doctor.

Now I remember... that's the kid... The truck! She's okay... He exhaled with relief for her, forgetting his own plight for the moment.

The doctor's words of assurance rang through Tony's thoughts, which made him think that the doctor was addressing him.

"She's fine--some bruises and scratches, and a bump that a little ice can relieve. She's a very lucky little girl."

Tony suddenly realized that the physician was not acknowledging him when he heard her father, who had pointed to the adjoining curtained bed, Tony's bed, and had asked with deep concern, "He didn't make it, did he?"

The nurse nodded agreement in silence. The man's face muscles tightened as tears fell from his eyes. With a look of disbelief, he asked the nurse his name. She answered with a hard swallow, "Anthony Romero, a stockbroker according to his business card." She glanced over to the still body and added in a whisper, "and now, a hero."

"Yes, indeed a hero," the father agreed with solemnity.

Tony, stung by the words, screamed to get their attention.

Hero? Me? he snorted. *Wait a minute, wait a minute, look! I'm fine, I'm here! Look! I'm going back!* he protested without recognition.

Without warning, he found himself once again hovering over his limp body. He still believed it was all a crazy dream. Some kind of a surreal nightmare.

The nurse covered his face with a bed sheet, and a feeling of loss overtook him. He made a futile attempt to undo his demise by frantic shouts down to his corpse.

Wake up! Wake up!

His words echoed as darkness began to fill the room. He felt a strong pull that drew him toward the glow of a light, through a portal, and into a tunnel of some sort. Its confines shimmered bright particles in colors of white, gold and red that circulated like the swirl of leaves under a forceful wind.

Engulfed, he whirled at lightning speed toward the bright core ahead without any sensation of fear. He looked back and saw the hospital room fade into blackness.

"Jumping Jack Frost!" he cried, feeling the thrill of acceleration. "But where am I going?"

He pinched himself, still convinced it was just a wild dream. "Boy, Freud would dig this. I'll have to write it all down for interpretation."

He rocketed, driven by an unseen energy, and became more exhilarated as he went on. However, he still clung to the hope that he would awaken. That is, until his flight took an abrupt halt, and he landed in a tumble on a stone path.

He got to his feet and found himself in a torch-lit cavern, standing at a fork in a path. The stones that made the walkway appeared glossed from centuries of wear. He stared about at his surroundings in silent wonder, until a noise caught his attention.

"What's that sound?" he murmured.

He heard inaudible voices coming from the left side of the path. "Sounds like a party," he said with a grin. He was about to take the left fork until he noticed a glimmer of golden light on the right side. He scratched his head, hardly believing what was going on.

"My God, this is strange. It's becoming more exotic." He shrugged. "I probably drank more than I thought, that's all." Tony decided to play into it as if it were an adventure game, and pondered the next move.

"I guess I'm required to make a choice here. Let's see, which fork I should take?" he pondered with another scratch of his head. With the belief that he was merely hallucinating, Tony was now a willing game participant.

He moved closer to the dividing point and the voices got louder; from the left fork, he heard his name called out in a tempting sweet voice.

"Come this way, Tony. Party with us!"

Another voice--a different, kinder one—followed, which beckoned him from the path to his right. "Anthony," a man's voice called. Tony looked carefully, but could not see where the mysterious voice had come from.

A form appeared on the path—a man in a white tuxedo. Tony squinted at the apparition of this tall, slimly-built person, all aglow in golden light. He generated an aristocratic demeanor, along with a kindness Tony had rarely experienced among his fellows.

The apparition addressed him once again. "Anthony, I've been sent for you. Your act of love for the child has done much to redeem your soul. Come, follow me to your future," he encouraged Tony as he reached out for him.

Befuddled, Tony followed, drawn by his certain, trustworthy charisma. He took the right fork in resistance to stronger appeals from the other. The instant Tony crossed over its threshold, he became completely aware of his death, and froze in place.

"Oh no, I'm...," he muttered, unable to complete the word of finality. His stomach churned with grief as the piercing reality of total separation from his earthly life became clear to him. His guide, though, continued to lead, allowing Tony no time to wallow in his misery.

The cavern widened, illuminated by the light that emanated from the man's body. In short time, Tony came to the edge of a tranquil body of water that sat under the glow of brilliant light.

The crystal-clear pool had polished granite pedestals on each of its sides. The mysterious man, his identity yet undisclosed, offered guidance as he pointed.

"Anthony, the pedestal at the right of you will purge you of your failings. Sit there first. The other will enlighten you to the good that God has given and done through you."

"Sir, am I not dreaming all this?"

"No, my brother, this is your true reality. The merciful bridge to eternal joy."

Still half believing that it was all a dream, he asked further, "My wife and children, will I see them again?"

"Yes, in time, but in a different light."

"Who are you?" Tony asked.

"My name is Pinchot, and I am your guardian. I have been with you since your earthly birth. Please sit, and as you reflect, everything will become clearer. Your spiritual memory will re-surface."

Tony, wary, his eyebrows raised, followed Pinchot's instructions and sat upon the first pedestal. When he did, the quiet pool transformed into a sparkling waterfall. It sprayed him, causing a tingling sensation.

The pool displayed three-dimensional images at its center. A vision formed of Tony at age seven. It showed him dressed in a Yankee baseball uniform, playing with his cousin. Tony saw his younger self push down the other boy and take away his toy. His cousin's response resounded from the depths of Tony's childhood:

"Hey, Anthony, you always do that! Why can't we share?"

"I don't want to share. If you want it so bad, fight me for it," Tony bullied back, with a fist in his cousin's face.

"I don't want to fight," the other boy said with a frown. "My mother said that you have a mean streak in you, and I don't like you anymore. You don't have to be that way. Why are you so?"

The interlude had begun to fade, but not before Tony took account of the forlorn look upon his cousin's face as it retracted from the scene. He recognized his selfishness, and that this part of him had taken root in his early years.

"I remember that. I know I felt bad for what I had done, but I chose to ignore it and kept the toy anyway. But why?" he asked, gazing at the waters of the pool.

Pinchot just nodded, letting similar visions progress. They abated when he sensed that Tony needed to dig into them with greater introspection.

The reflective images of Tony's prior life continued to unfold. He saw himself and his pattern of behavior in greater clarity, the worst being that of a self-serving predator. Given these insights, he squirmed with the realization of the hurt he had wrought upon so many.

He became keenly and painfully aware now that he had not expressed an abundance of love to his family, mostly to his wife. Not to mention the countless others he had encountered on earth. He now felt the depth of their respective feelings and the pain he had caused them.

Despondent, Tony fell to his knees before the pool, with unstoppable tears that cascaded into the water. When the drops made contact, they transformed into sparkling diamonds that penetrated his eyes with their brightness. In contrition, he stretched his arms over the glimmering pool.

"Oh my God, I am so sorry!" he bellowed with profound sadness.

At that moment, the unbearable weight of remorse he had carried lifted, replaced by a warm, awesome peace.

"Pinchot, are you still here?" he called, relief in his voice.

"Yes, Anthony. I'm here, as always."

"I know you now. I saw how you worked to turn me around, and I thank you for that. You never gave up on me." Tony shook his head. "It must have been frustrating for you."

Pinchot chuckled. "You are a definite handful. However, you will soon see that it was not just I who stood by you. Come now, the other pedestal waits. There you will see how our Creator has gifted you.

"Be guided by the words of an insightful mind from your time. Mystic George Gurdjieff once stated, *Self-observation brought man to the realization of the necessity of self-change, and that with self-observation a man noticed that it brought about change in his inner processes... the means of awakening.*"

Six

PINCHOT PLACED HIS HAND upon Tony's still-trembling shoulder and coaxed him to sit on the second pedestal.

In a flash, Tony found himself in a chariot of sorts, seated upon lush red velvet cushions with Pinchot happily beside him.

In a thrust, the coach careened over the water and plunged beneath the waterfall. Tony instinctively held his breath, though to his surprise he did not need to. He inhaled and exhaled comfortably, without any sensation of choking or being wet. As the volume of water contacted his skin, he merely experienced a tingling sensation. He massaged his arm in disbelief.

In a microsecond, they were through to the other side, dry and in view of a magical panorama. They began to make their way through a lush valley, guarded by pink snow-capped mountains that hugged lakes and streams which abounded with life. Amazed at the sight of it, Tony gasped in wonder.

"Pinchot...may I call you that?"

Pinchot nodded.

"I feel part of all the life around me."

The plants, insects, and animals all spoke to him in some way. There were species known to him, and others exotic and unfamiliar. After experiencing the embrace of such wonder, Tony's concerns were now on hold.

"Pinchot, do you hear that? They're telling me their histories since the time of creation." Tony pointed. "Listen, it's speaking to me. The big white one."

"Greetings to you, creation of God. I am what you call in the human realm a 'flower', akin to an earthly orchid. The countless varieties of we who abide in heaven's realms have been gifted with intelligence and are capable of intention and preference." That said, it opened its petals and exuded an indescribable perfumed scent.

"Wow!" Tony said, as a burst of fragrance visited his nostrils. Pinchot smiled as the exotic flower bowed in acknowledgement of Tony's response.

A reddish fern planted at its side spoke up. "Welcome, human creation. I am a velvet fern, one also of unlimited varieties. We plants communicate with insects, animals, human beings, and other plants in order to sustain them with God's gift of pleasure and joy." Then it laughed. "No poison ivy or oak here. No need for survival defenses in heaven. Their texture oozes love when touched," it said, as it waved a branch in farewell.

Tony could only stare silently into the distance.

"Yes, Anthony. All aspects of creation are in a natural harmony, fitting together despite individual complexities."

Without warning, the chariot catapulted. It soared high above the peaks and climbed upward and upward, out into deep space. Tony braced himself, exhilarated but apprehensive, like a child experiencing his first rollercoaster ride.

The excitement of the ride was diminished only by his amazement as he found himself at the center of the Milky Way Galaxy. "Wow!" he said as he pointed.

"Look, Pinchot! I can see the Earth there, housed within a myriad of stars and planets, and they all seem to work together. Amazing."

The coach slowed at the sight of an emerging new galaxy. Its awesome energy was evident as it birthed stars and planets through its womb of life, all the time expelling colorful gases as witness to its embryonic creation.

"It's mind-boggling,' Tony whispered, agog. "Every molecule is taking on voice, even the planets and moons. Pinchot, there are no words that can express this. My God, how small and insignificant we are."

"What's even more amazing," Pinchot offered with a parental tap on Tony's shoulder, "is that you and your fellow man have dominion over it all. It is your gift. A gift once held by humanity, but squandered in disobedience in the Garden of Eden. By the way, it wasn't about the apple. It was a matter of trust. Ponder that."

In a flash, they were back at the limpid pool, and Tony sat reunited with the pedestal once more, staring at the waterfall. This time the images of his gifts and talents began to unfold before him.

In experiencing this vision, he recognized his abilities and accomplishments. He gained understanding of his life passage from his early years, and saw now that he had possessed a certain charisma, augmented by an innate ability for leadership—a respected motivator, one who made things happen.

Tony had the ability to gain the trust of colleagues, employees, and stakeholders. He showed them his devotion and commitment to completing tasks, no matter how many hours it took. He built his business by analyzing the needs of his prospective clients.

In this time of personal inventory, he saw how he had listened to his clients, how he had respected their views and ideas, and with painstaking research he had presented his ideas, growing their trust. He had created and developed fresh ideas while maintaining the core values of a project, all the while maintaining a sense of humor and staying focused. One of his greatest gifts was the ability to make decisions based on logic and fact, thus gaining the confidence of others.

He learned how well planned and focused his skills were, combined with his ability to sell a point of view with confidence. These revelations were most profound for him. He saw God's hand in his life, a revelation that brought him once more to his knees before the pool, this time with gratefulness. His tears met the water and transformed into precious jewels that lit up with a golden hue.

Pinchot took Tony by the hand and explained with pastoral certainty, "Anthony, the Creator in His infinite love and mercy has rained down the sanctified water of repentance and joy contained in this pool. It was first shed in sacrifice by your ancestors, collected and purified here, then given back to humanity in the form of grace."

Tony nodded, though he struggled to understand and find words.

Pinchot guided him to yet another portal.

"Does this mean I'm going into heaven now?"

"I wish I had a musical note for every time I heard that question." Pinchot laughed softly. "I'd have a symphony, akin to Mozart's Symphony no. 40.

"Anthony, you are already in heaven. Just, let us say, on the outer fringe. Your journey now continues in a place where your precious being will be purged of imperfections by prayer and reflection."

"I guess I'm going to Purgatory?"

"Well some call it that; I prefer to think of it as what you would call 'boot camp'," he quipped, enjoying his own wit with a chuckle.

"Your precious metals on earth are purged in fire to give them strength. You, also, will be purged in the fire of the Holy Spirit to realize yours," Pinchot instructed with a respectful bow of his head.

Moving on, they passed through a portal of plasma-like material into the light of day. A stone walkway appeared beneath their feet, glistening over a body of radiance. Tony tested it with his foot, in the way a curious child would do, which caused more light to surface.

The walkway, edged with greenery and flora of all kinds, blanketed everything with abounding brightness. He mused in his mind with affection.

Norma would love this. She always amazed me with her design ability and use of color. Then he shook his head in remorse. *She not only brought color into our house, but into our lives.*

He knew that he had dimmed them for her, had taken the vibrancy right out of her heart. Now he worried about her wellbeing. Tony's mind filled with a mixed bag of concern and awe, plus an admiration of her beautiful soul, that he had discounted and taken for granted.

I was a real jerk.

He gazed up at the sky and pointed with surprise to an abundant variety of exotic winged creatures, most unknown to him. Tony waved to them, as a child would, drawn by their majesty and beauty. However, inside he remained weighted down, feeling unworthy and unentitled to experience such beauty.

He thought of his kids, and how he had failed them. *They always wanted to have a bird, and I canned the idea with lame excuses.*

In his heart, he asked their forgiveness, cognizant that his focus had always centered on himself, his goals and needs, not those of his family or others. This revelation convicted him as a selfish fool, an introspection that indeed prepared him for the pending isolation, discomfort, and spiritual purging of Purgatory.

In the near distance, a path unfolded that led into another illuminated valley. A vibrant green expanse surrounded a gem-like village, and at its center sat a castle shaded in a red hue.

Tony's mouth hung open in astonishment. *Wow! It just jumps out at you, its design and the way it shimmers rainbows of light.*

"That's Paraclete City. It is beautiful, isn't it?" Pinchot offered, as if reading his mind. Tony concurred with a speechless nod.

"There you will encounter your family members who, in a way, are part of your orientation. I will be leaving you there," he said, preparing him.

"Leave me? I thought you were my Guardian."

"Yes, don't worry. I am your Guardian and always will be. Whenever you want me, just bring me to mind and I will be there. But, for now, I place you in the care of your mentor who, like yourself, is of human origin and of free will."

"Mentor?"

"Well, I guess another word for it would be Spiritual Director or Guide." He stopped himself. "Hmm, 'guide'... That's an ambiguous term, fondly adopted by your so-called 'new age' contemporaries."

As they approached the city, they found themselves joining a line of souls in human form, accompanied by their respective winged Guardians. Pinchot embraced his angelic counterparts in loving acknowledgement. Tony noticed that when the angels made physical contact with each other, a tremendous burst of energy exchanged between them.

They each introduced their charges, and pleasant conversation was made.

Although the line consisted of hundreds, somehow all, in short order, assembled in front of a jeweled Administrator's desk, regally embossed with the image of an ivory dove. Behind it sat a nun in a brilliant magenta cloak.

"Another one through, Pinchot," she attested, coming from behind the desk to greet him.

"Praise is to God for you, Yasodmuni. God is glorified with the wonder of your soul," he said. He embraced her and set off another astounding explosion of light and energy.

"Praise is to God for you, Anthony Romero. Welcome," Yasodmuni, a lighthearted Buddhist nun said, as she embraced him. He embraced her back, expecting a dose of energy, but remained dimly lit, like a waning light bulb.

Amazed by it all, he did not speak. He merely bowed, happily enjoying the glow of joy he received by her touch.

"Pinchot, you know the drill...you're assigned the hall at Plateau IX."

Pinchot nodded.

"Anthony, Sister Rose Margaret will escort you to the banquet." She handed him a deep purple cloak. It dazzled his eyes; this shade was a deeper purple than any he had ever seen on earth. That remembered color paled amongst the exquisite ones that now surrounded him.

Sister continued, "I am excited for you. Your journey to perfect peace and joy is underway. Take courage. As our Lord has shown, pain is the stepping stone to ultimate joy."

Pain? Tony repeated in his thoughts. *What pain?*

The reality of his fate began to surface.

Seven

THEY EXITED THROUGH ornate bronze elevator doors embossed with images of angels. Tony, dazed by it all, arrived in a large foyer. Gold-framed paintings of the Saints lined its walls and called to his eye.

"This is the Hall of Saints," Pinchot confirmed. At once Tony heard his name called.

"Praise is to God for you, Anthony. Welcome!" a robust, veiled woman greeted him. She then addressed Pinchot.

"Praise is to God for you, Pinchot; blessed is your name and Choir of your brethren."

He nodded. "Devoted Sister Rose Margaret, safe-keeper of souls."

Sister Rose Margaret, a joyful soul herself, was dressed in a tunic of magenta, with patterns that mimicked the frolicking nature of angels. She tickled Pinchot under his chin with her finger, causing him to blush.

"Anthony," Sister said, displaying an impish grin, "I will come to retrieve you after your banquet. All of your guests are looking forward to the lasagna." With a heartfelt laugh, she added with a hum, "Being of Italian extraction myself, lasagna was a ritual in our familial home."

She giggled, jingling a long garnet rosary belted about her waist. "Enjoy. I will return to you, my brother."

Tony swallowed. `*My brother'... wow.* This was the first that he'd realized his connection to the citizens of the heavenly realm.

He waited with anticipation, and wondered whom he would meet, and about the prospect of his first other-worldly meal. Confused, he shook his head.

Lasagna... a banquet? Welcomed into Purgatory with a banquet? This is incredible.

"Anthony, there's going to be a slight delay," Pinchot told him. "I'll just be a minute; wait for me there by the golden doors."

Tony complied, but lent his ear with curiosity as Pinchot enquired of Sister Rose.

"Blessed Sister..."

The jolly nun stopped him short with a knowing smile. "I know what you're going to ask. Yes, I felt it too. When exactly did you sense it?"

"As I stepped upon the path with Tony. It became stronger as we proceeded here."

"Yes, it's been quite strong here. Unsettling, is it not? I guess we'll just have to let it unfold."

"Yes, of course," he said with a respectful bow. He then stepped back next to Tony, who had focused on a plaque that hung beside the large golden doors.

"Plateau 6, Hall of Archangel Pinchot, Guardian of Souls," he read aloud as Pinchot joined him. "I guess you're a famous guy; it says here that you have served the

Lord God from the time of His manifestation, whatever that may mean. I guess I should be honored, having an Archangel at my side."

"Oh, come on Tony. How do you say it...'give me a break'?" His face though, registered proud with the recognition.

Pinchot exhibited his supernatural power; with a hand motion, the majestic doors opened, gaining them access to the elevator. Inside, its spacious interior was hung with Middle Eastern-styled tapestries that depicted scenes of cherubs frolicking with celestial animal life.

A screeching sound, akin to a tape running on fast-forward, brought Tony's hands to his ears.

"Is that the sound of the elevator movement?"

"No, no..." Pinchot chuckled, "It's a 'linger'."

Tony just stared at him.

"You see," Pinchot explained, "here we have the ability to do a recall of sorts. You know, like an instant replay in your previous world.

"Angels have great curiosity and interest in humans. Also, deep admiration for the wonder of your creation; we find you quite fascinating, to say the least. Your sense of comedy is, you'd say... a gas." He giggled.

Tony laughed, though still dumbfounded. He encouraged him with a hand motion to keep talking.

"I believe someone, prior to exiting, shared something very funny. Most likely one of our Angelic number who wanted to 'linger' in the joy of it, but probably so taken in laughter, he left it playing."

Tony shook his head in disbelief. It was inconceivable to him at that point to think that Angels would find the human species so compelling. He viewed them as powerful, supernatural beings with astounding abilities.

He did not realize that Angels viewed humans as beings of privilege who shared in God's creation, that they regarded mortals as royal children, Princes and Princesses of God's Kingdom.

Tony's imagination was piqued about this ability to 'linger', and he searched Pinchot for further insight.

"To engage it, one must first recall a few words, or a phrase, and mouth them. In doing so, the audio scene will automatic re-play on a frequency and a speed of choice."

Tony stopped him. "Are you saying that all the people who are here, and I venture to say, numbered in the billions, have frequencies of their own?"

"Well, I guess you may say that. Think about what your scientists call the 'black hole'. They theorize that matter is sucked in and condensed into a small, dense molecule. If all that can be contained in a particle, then accordingly why not a multitude of frequencies? You're not thinking large here, Anthony."

He laughed and went on.

"Let me get back to the 'linger' for the moment; it will be useful for you in your stay here. It stops when one repeats the sentence or when it plays out. However, it is more, *pronounced*, encased in the elevator. I guess you noticed that it just stopped."

Tony laughed with the oddity of it all.

The elevator doors opened to the sight of a massive empty ballroom. As they exited the elevator, Tony, still curious about what he had overheard between Pinchot and the Sister, asked if what they had been discussing had something to do with a 'linger'.

Suddenly thinking that it may have been out of place to ask, he sought pardon. "Am I being intrusive?"

"No... no...," Pinchot answered, "Heavens... no... there are no secrets here, just things to learn. The matter I visited with Blessed Sister concerned a certain unusual feeling. An unforeseen disruption of some kind I suppose, one that I experienced when we arrived in close proximity to Paraclete City. She confessed having had a similar sensation, and now we wait to discern God's intention, which can only be right and just."

Tony massaged his head and wondered how a disruption in heaven could possibly happen. His eyes surveyed the ballroom, especially its exotic wood floor, inlaid with a bright gold cross that pulsated as if alive.

Amazed once again, he thought, *The Queen of England herself would feel diminished in a room such as this.* He circled the room with his eyes, and at once felt even more unentitled at the sight of its grandeur. Still in amazement, he pointed to its Romanesque walls of three-dimensional paintings.

Archangel Pinchot offered with pride, "The frescoes depict my brother and sister angels in their original celestial choirs: Seraphim, Cherubim, Thrones, Dominions, Virtues, Powers, Principalities, and mine--Archangels. A blessed and glorious tribute to Him who Is and always will Be. Creation's infinite well of eternal love and mercy."

The vast empty room also gave off a perfumed aroma, similar to the scent of gardenia, which he remembered as his mother's favorite. This prompted another sad recollection, bringing to mind his separation from his parents and adding to the hollowness left inside at the absence of Norma and his children.

I failed all of them.

Pinchot broke into his introspection with the joyful announcement that the affair was about to begin. In preparation, he gave Tony the low down.

"I should give you a brief explanation concerning physical contact. You see, many of them, your guests, are already in a glorified state, while your being, presently, does not yet contain the fullness of the Holy Spirit. Some will embrace you, but let them take the lead, so to speak."

Tony scratched his head as he stood in the empty hall, fidgeting, not knowing who or what to expect. He asked himself, *Why can I touch Pinchot? He leads me by the hand...*

Pinchot read confusion on his face and offered a further explanation. "I know. It may be strange at this point. However, you may ponder this." He highlighted that angels did not rule--that they shared free will with humans, but their state of creation was different.

"Our beloved Paul of Tarsus taught with these prophetic words, and I quote: *So, while mankind was given dominion only over the physical creation in this system of things, he will be given dominion even over the heavenly creations in the Kingdom of God.*

Tony's mind spun with puzzlement. He followed Pinchot to a table at the head of the room, one extravagantly set. In wonder, he reached out his hands and explored the gold-embossed dishes and delicate engraved utensils as a child would. He admired the exquisitely woven, pastel-colored linens, which dressed the countless tables in the room.

He looked about and wondered why no one had joined them, which played into his lingering dream theory. He was still incredulous that such an admitted sinner as he would be received with such grandeur--a soul on the precipice of a penitential stay in Purgatory.

In a moment, like the click of a remote control, his guests appeared in a receiving line before his table. The first were his grandparents, dressed in bronze-colored silky tunics, exhibiting auras that showed their joy.

He rushed with excitement to embrace them, but stopped when, instead, they extended their arms and projected beams of light. These touched Tony and gave him the warm sensation of a kiss.

"Praise is to God for you, our beloved grandson," his grandmother welcomed. "We have been praying and waiting for you. Soon you will have the full joy of eternal peace. We are so proud of the many good things you have done. Giving your life to save another is the most anyone can do for a child of God.

"There are so many here who wish to welcome you. Enjoy your banquet. The Celestial Chef used my recipe for the lasagna; I am sure it is now much improved." She laughed. "We will meet again when you pass through the Great Gate of Glory."

The couple blew him golden kisses. They embraced Pinchot with gratitude, producing electrostatic claps, and made for their assigned table.

Pinchot continued to introduce Tony to generations of relatives, which all seemed to happen in a moment of time. Angelic waiters served plates filled with fragrant tempting foods, and his guests thanked God for every morsel and every sip of fine wine they ingested.

A bell rang, and all raised their glasses to Tony, who burst into tears.

"This is all incredible. I just don't feel..."

"Worthy?" Pinchot finished the sentence for him.

"That's just it, Anthony. No one is worthy of God's infinite love and mercy."

He indicated the food before him. "Eat, Anthony--the music and dancing are about to start."

Tony felt a vibration of energy, as the walls moved to allow a stage to form before the expansive dance floor. Music filtered in with melodies contemporary of Tony's time. The smiling, well-dressed guests took to the dance floor.

He saw the sparkle of those assembled--tuxedos that shimmered on the musicians, the luster of their exotic instruments, and the vibrant robes of the guests. They all shared a common demeanor.

They are natural. Theirs is a heartfelt love, with a noticeable absence of vanity and guile--everyone and everything in communion. His eyes welled up tears, and his heart with a greater appreciation of God's love.

The joyful affair went on for an incalculable length of time. When the guests began to take their leave, they sent more golden kisses, which electrified him and filled him with an accumulation of spiritual sustenance.

The stage, musicians and all, dematerialized and the room dimmed, leaving him once again alone with Pinchot.

"Well, Anthony, were you pleased by your welcome celebration?"

"Pleased? It was the most magnificent experience of my life, Pinchot. I just don't understand. Why me? I was such a dog, and hurtful, above all to my wife."

"Blessed Sister Rose Margaret will soon join us. She will guide you to the place where the purging process will begin for you. It is there that you will find true understanding, reconciliation, and God's purpose for you."

"Are you leaving me?"

"Yes. I pray to meet you at the Great Gate, with your family, when in time you arrive there for the ultimate celebration. For now, I re-join my Choir to bask in the presence of Him, the Creator of Infinite Love."

With that, Pinchot transformed into an angelic form of indescribable beauty, dressed in a dazzling golden robe. He sprouted huge, velvety-soft wings of brilliant white and his height extended to nine feet. Tony shook in awe as the angel reached down to pat him, sending a shockwave of joy into his being.

Sister Rose Margaret appeared in a silvery cloud.

"Oh, Glorious Archangel Pinchot, peace and joy are yours." Her voice carried to him as he ascended into a beacon of light above. The light engulfed him as his voice echoed down in response, "Eternal peace and joy to you, blessed sister."

Tony felt hollow inside as he assumed a more earthlike emotional state. Concerned now, he gave his attention to the nun's words of counsel.

"Anthony, you received a red carpet welcome with a banquet, and were shown much love. This welcome will build in intensity when you allow yourself to enter the City of God."

Tony nodded as the good sister continued to prepare him.

"The Holy Spirit will inform and challenge your will," she told him, but also assured him that the Spirit would help him to arbitrate the contributing elements that stood between him and his ultimate peace of Heaven's Realm.

At that point, the spirit within made it known to Tony what lay ahead; what he would experience through human feelings again, though more intense than ever before. His memories of good and bad would become clearer, more pronounced, edifying him with equal portions of pain and joy.

Sister Rose Margaret took his hand. "Allow yourself to accept the challenge, for in that you will find eternal peace."

Apprehensive now, Tony was skeptical and unsure of his ability to change. He questioned once more why God would entertain any interest in him.

His trepidation festered as Sister Rose led him through another set of doors and down a long corridor to an elevator of sorts; in actuality, a platform open on all sides, which he stepped upon with uncertainty.

"Anthony, there are nine levels, leading to the bowels of Hell. You will experience an assortment of feelings and you may even see souls that you have known in your past life. They may call out to you."

With a foreboding stir in his voice he asked, "Sister Rose, so it is true that God punishes us for what we have done in our lives?"

"Blessed Son of the Holy One, this is a place of penitence; however, God did not assign anyone here. Eternal damnation, my brother, is not of God's initiative, because in His merciful love He desires the salvation of all beings of His creation. The reality is that the souls here have closed themselves off from God's love, either in part or entirely."

Sister's words conjoined with newly-received information implanted now into his psyche. The Spirit gave him the capability to make an assessment with theological wisdom.

He reflected upon the idea that damnation existed as a definitive separation from God, freely chosen by the human person and confirmed with death. One that sealed that person's choice forever. God's judgment sanctioned this state, however unpleasant it may be for Him.

Tony picked up the odor of sulfur, panicked, and asked in a trembling voice, "So how long will I be here?"

"That will be all up to you, with the aid of prayers by souls on earth and the saints that abide in Paradise. In here, there are different levels; the lowest one being Hell and the highest being on the precipice of Heaven."

Tony stirred, disappointed with himself, as her words sank in. His stomach soured as he became aware that he had discounted God his entire life. His thoughts were amplified by a superimposed vision of Christ's crucifixion.

Sister continued her orientation, "It is not on All Souls Day, but at Christmas, that the greatest numbers of souls are graduated to a higher level or released from here."

Tony listened with keen ears as the nun explained that souls who prayed in ardent fervor to God, especially those who have no living relative or friend to pray for them on Earth, were allowed by God to benefit from the anonymous prayers of other people.

Tony thought of his wife again. *I hope Norma is praying for me.*

Sister Rose went on to tell him that God permitted some souls in transition to manifest themselves in different ways to those closest to them on earth. This He did to remind man of the existence of Purgatory and to solicit their prayers. As a result, this would expedite union with Him, Who is just and merciful.

Tony's eyes widened at the prospect of seeing his family.

"Like us, a majority of souls go to Purgatory, though many unfortunately also go to Hell. A smaller number have a direct path to Heaven."

"So I guess it's true that Hell exists."

She educated him as church theologians would. "A soul," she told him, stopping to inhale, "in taking the risk of saying 'yes' or 'no,' marks the human creature's freedom, his free will.

"Those who have already said no," she continued, "are the spiritual creatures that have rebelled against God's love, who we know as demons."

Tony opened his lips to speak, but Sister Rose answered as if she had read his mind.

"No, Anthony, you are not bound for Hell," she told him, and made the sign of the cross. "Due to my own failings, I am grateful I just missed it. You, however, have been blessed with a start at Level I, a place where glimpses of heaven can be seen from time to time, and where heavenly citizens may visit to encourage those who dwell there. The precipice of heaven." Then she added with mystery, "But you are also given a special challenge."

Tony wondered, *Top level? Special challenge?*

Sister continued with her orientation. "There are several levels in Purgatory. The more you pray on earth, the higher your level in Purgatory will be. The lowest level is the closest to hell, where the suffering is the most intense. The highest level is closest to Heaven, and there the suffering is the least. What level you are on depends on the state of purity of your soul.

"The lower the level people are on in Purgatory, the less they are able to pray and the more they suffer. The higher the level a person is in Purgatory, the easier it is for them to pray, and the more he enjoys praying. Therefore, the less he suffers."

Tony sighed with relief; he'd be saved from viewing hell when they landed at the deepest level of Purgatory.

This level was a cold abyss obscured in a gray fog the color of burnt ash. One could say that it was like sitting in a boat that floated in a haze, where sky and sea showed no definition. Uncountable waves of people, which he sensed but was unable to see, crowded together, all scurrying in a frantic back and forth, like those in New York's Grand Central Station.

He caught glimpses of their translucent spirit form where they stayed close to scattered vents of fire, seeking some warmth. Tony tried to shield his eyes from this dismal scene. He also covered his ears to damper the sounds of people, weeping and groaning in what seemed like terrible suffering.

"Oh my God, Sister... There are... peop... people I know. What have they done to warrant this?"

"Willful, grievous sin of the worst kind, Tony, like cold-blooded murder. They have turned away from God, and have broken His Commandments with regularity. Worse, though, is that they distrusted His love and mercy."

Those known to Tony reached out to him, petitioning his prayer, hungry for relief. He felt their desperation and pain, and was frustrated in not being able to help them. He attempted to shield his eyes with his hands, but still saw right through them.

"Sister Rose, please," he begged, his voice trembling, overtaken by their grief. "Please... Sister, please take me from here," he repeated. As he said this, his own words reminded him of Ebenezer Scrooge, who had pleaded to the dark Christmas Spirit in the same words.

Sister remained quiet as the elevator climbed over the echoed shouts for prayer. Thusly they visited each level, with the same pleading result from Tony. As they disembarked at the top level, into another space that defied definition, he found himself immersed in a fog. It was like the others, but thinner and lighter in color, with streaks of light able to penetrate its misty, foreboding clouds.

The voices he heard there were calmer. Casting his eyes about, he saw shadows of figures through the misty gray air.

Eight

THEY ARRIVED AT A GAZEBO-like structure. A slightly-built teenage boy, around fourteen, awaited them. He was long-faced and awkward, with drooping shoulders. Sister Rose Margaret introduced Tony. "Anthony, this is Obe..."

"Praise is to God for you, kind bride of the Son," he answered, with a probing look at Tony.

"Anthony, you have been assigned to the guidance of Obe--Obermyer Coddington--and him to you." Tony scrutinized the small-proportioned teenager who stood before him. His face was ashen and his large eyes sad, but his visage shifted once they were introduced.

"Welcome to your last stop before Heaven," he announced, with a grin and a brush of his dark-brown hair. Sister Rose raised her eyebrows at his theatrics.

"Is something happening up there?" Obe inquired of her, indicating the area where Tony had first entered eternity.

"I guess you feel it here too. Does everyone feel it?"

"No, I think just me. What be it then?"

"We don't know. Many are feeling it, even the Choirs. We have not been enlightened. In actuality, I feel it more here."

Obe shook his head as his smoky gray eyes captured Tony. "Follow me, brother."

Sister offered Tony some motherly advice before they departed.

"My brother, apply everything you can with every ounce and force of will. My prayers are with you."

Tony took in her sympathetic eyes, and saluted with a bow of the head. He followed the young man who, like himself, wore a purple robe, but with the exception that it had a gold band on its right sleeve.

In the denseness of the vast ashen space, they approached an immense portal encircled by a large number of shadows, which Obe explained were those of penitent souls. They joined them to peer down over its edge, and saw a spectacular view of the earth, as if viewed out the window of a spacecraft.

"This is what we call the Well of Hope--our lifeline. Through it we can receive prayer for our redemption," young Obe told him.

While looking over, Tony brushed against some of the others gathered there, and felt sensations of their pain, causing him to pull back. "What was that?" he asked Obe.

"We all carry a level of discomfort here. When you touch another, theirs adds to yours."

"You're right. I do feel pain, and it is increasing, like a constant aching all over my being."

"Just imagine what that feels like in the lower levels. Praise is to God that you are not there. It is much darker, and the souls confined there experience severe unceasing pain. They shiver, thrash, and lament in unrelenting discomfort, and because of it they are unable to pray."

"Oh my God, yes. I saw that. I just visited there. A horrendous place."

The sad young man pointed to a stone bench hardly distinguishable through the mist.

"Let us sit there and we will share our stories."

They sat. Tony, becoming overwhelmed and somewhat frenzied, barked out, "How long will I be here?"

"That depends upon what prayer offerings you receive, and the way your heart changes in conjunction with them."

"What did Sister Rose mean when she told me to 'apply everything I can with every ounce and force of my will'?"

"Oh, Our Lord, the Great Redeemer of Souls, in His Divine Mercy, allows us to pray more comfortably here at this level. However, we depend greatly on those who have known us, loved us on the earth. And most importantly on those who pray blindly for lost souls, through the Holy Mass and their personal prayer."

"Does this mean I can contact them?"

"Yes, in a way, by your prayer, but they have to be predisposed to it. You know, open to it."

"Tell me, what was that whole banquet thing about? Why the celebration, if I was to come here?"

"Banquet? Wake up and see the sunrise here; miracles happen. You saw into the pool. You reviewed your passage through life and, like most of us here, probably saw it as contrary and self-seeking, I venture to guess.

Nonetheless, your strong belief in God and the times you answered His call to do the right thing were enough to override your errors. Maybe God sees something wonderful that can blossom in you. Your awareness of waiting family will indeed help you cope with this separation from God."

"How did you know all that?"

"All of us are disclosed in heaven's realms."

"So then, with all that, why am I here?"

Obe did not answer. He knew that for most souls, their thirst for money and selfishness betrayed the special gifts that God created in them. Moreover, because of it, they ignored the emotional, physical, and spiritual needs of others.

They isolated themselves from God and relegated Him to a concept relying upon less-than-heartfelt ritual prayer, which watered down its meaning. Either that, or they wavered in their belief of Him, albeit nominally involved in said belief.

"Maybe you were a selfish jerk?"

Tony stomped his foot. "Hey wait a minute!" he barked, then winced from a sudden increased pain.

"Relax, Tony. The more wrath you allow, the more discomfort you will feel. If you want to get out of here, acceptance and trust are the words to ponder."

With an edged surety, Obe went on to share his belief that God invited him, and all of creation, to a relationship. He also shared that God's infinite love stood ready to be tapped into, but that each individual had the choice to accept or reject it.

He added, with a dramatic outstretch of his arms, "It's as clear as a headline."

Tony, calmer now, said, "You're right Obe. You know, I have always loved God. I had fear of Him in my youth, especially in Catholic school, but I always felt that He'd be with me. I also know now that Pinchot stood by my side every step of the way. I believe he guided me away from making worse decisions. I am grateful for that."

"Pinchot? Archangel Pinchot?" Obe's mouth hung open for a moment. "For his love of God, he is only second to Archangel Michael! You've been in great company. Maybe I should ask you for a political favor," he laughed.

Obe experienced a jolt of pain, and elevated his eyes to excuse himself.

"Just kidding."

"How do you know my story?"

Obe explained that the Redeemer bestowed this knowledge upon each of them there, in the penitential realm, so that they might help one another focus introspectively; reality checks, so to speak, on why and how they had arrived in Purgatory, and the spiritual work before them.

Tony, still curious and trying to find his way, asked Obe what this "odd sensation" was that he had heard Sister speak of, both to him and Pinchot.

Obe paused in thought, not knowing if it was appropriate for him to discuss it, but took the risk of another zap.

"Well, you see, Tony, we are experiencing something inside that seems to be affecting the order of things. We do not know if it is good or bad--it is just...different."

What Obe did not say was that the citizens of the heavenly realm were usually too enmeshed in God's love to experience anything disturbing or negative. In fact, for Obe, that it existed at all made it even more confounding. Especially because he was the only soul, in their present state of consciousness, that had begun to experience it.

"What does it feel like?" Tony probed.

"I guess I can explain it this way. Picture this: we are all circuits on a grid in a supercomputer, part of a matrix attached to a central network and in constant communication--in this case, with God. We are in direct uninterrupted communication with Him.

"However, there now exists, what you may call static--a bug, that is. Like computer chips, we receive the signals, but the reception is disturbed now by a distractive interference. Something like a spiritual virus, a schism, if you will. We just have to wait and see."

Obe's narrative was interrupted by another soul, who appeared out of the mist.

"Prayers are for you, Obermyer Coddington," he announced.

"Prayers also for you, Zachariah Thomas." Obe introduced the newcomer. "Anthony Romero, this is Brother Zach. We were known to each other in our time on earth."

"Prayers are for you, Anthony Romero." The small-framed man greeted Tony with the energetic presence of a jockey.

Tony answered in kind, for the first time, "Prayers are for you too, Brother Zach."

"Brother Obe, there are prayers coming for you through the Well of Hope. If you wish, I will sit with Brother Anthony as you collect them."

"My thanks, Brother Zach." He waved and disappeared into the mist.

Brother Zach sat next to Tony and related pieces of his history with Obe. He explained with affection that he viewed Obe as a special soul, one with a profound love for God who should have made the final transition long ago. He winced with a pain of sadness for him, and further explained that Obe's life on earth was one of extreme suffering, adding with admiration that Obe had never lost his faith.

"Why is he still here?" Tony asked with curiosity.

"He has what you would call a 'dispute' with God."

"What?"

"Yes, one that started in his youth, even before the suffering befell him."

"How can one argue with God?"

"That's the crux of it, Brother Anthony."

The man went on to tell him that Obe had guided many a soul to the Great Gates, and they in turn had attempted to assist him with his reconciliation with God, but to no avail.

Tony repeated with disbelief, "How can anyone argue with God? God will always win, even I know that."

"Exactly. The thought of it makes me tremble."

The simple man went on to explain that he and Obe were colonial Southern Baptists who had attended the same parish church. Both were members of farm families. That, for the most part, he had seen Obe at Sunday service, where many times Obe's parents had to restrain him from questioning the pastor's homily and challenging his words publicly.

The man elaborated with ironic laughter, "Most offensive were the ones that wrought admonishment, the old-fashioned 'fire and brimstone'." Zach expounded further by making the crazy sign with a twirl of his finger, and received a jolt.

"There he'd be on any given Sunday, shouting from his seat at the pastor in disagreement. At other times, when greater dander consumed him, he'd make his way with that bounce-and-rock step of his to challenge him at the altar rail. He felt compelled to remind the preacher and the congregation of God's infinite love and mercy. Indeed a sight to see.

"The Pastor referred to him as his 'thorn of St. Paul'. At my young age I found it quite amusing, to the chagrin of my parents."

Tony was about to respond, but held his tongue as Zach suggested they harvest prayers at the well of hope themselves

"It's like checking one's mail box," he giggled, pleased by his use of modern-day language--although it caused him to flinch with increased pain, a celestial reminder for him not to detract from his task. "As you can see, humor is not high on the acceptable behavior list here," he said, and received another jolt.

Nine

HEAVEN BUZZED as some of its citizens awoke from a chosen period of absorption in God, what humans would associate with sleep or a meditative state. Time did not exist here. The new arrivals soon adjusted to the obvious absence of time and the exclusion of night or darkness of any kind. They only related to time in recall of their progressive life's journey.

Angels, and those pets who abided with them, playfully waited with song and joviality as they came to consciousness. One of whom, Mason Pringle, a learned citizen, regained consciousness to find a kink in heaven's fabric.

"Praise is to God for you, Mason Pringle."

"And also to you, blessed Angel Cornelael. What news do you bring?" he probed, his face and hands aglow.

"Oh my goodness... dear friend Mason Pringle... oh my goodness," he repeated with anguish.

"What is it, Cornelael?"

"You mean you don't feel it? The disruption?"

"Hmm...You know, I do. I did feel a little off as I re-entered this perfection. Yes! Oh my, yes. I do feel it, and did feel it before, now that you mention it." Mason nodded. "I guess that's why I chose to enjoin in the Lord," the distinguished-looking man surmised. He considered this while massaging his silver-gray beard, a look of curiosity upon his face.

"Off? Oh, kind and loving friend...that's just it. We don't feel 'off' here. This can never be a place of feeling 'off,'" the Archangel answered, reacting with heightened anxiety.

Mason continued to contemplate the phenomenon as he tied his gold-braided belt around his vibrant blue robe.

Scratching his frosted beard once again, he mused, "Yes, it is, curious, isn't it, but I'm sure Our Supreme Majesty has His reasons. We must trust and let His purpose unfold."

Pringle reached out to touch Cornelael's shoulder in assurance, but realized he had to levitate himself to do so.

"There... sometimes I forget how tall you are. But we are in perfect synch. I am five foot nine, and you are nine foot five."

They laughed heartedly. Then the prominent elder continued to speak with great affection. "You, my dear and loving friend, are what we call on earth, a worrier. In fact," he added with another bellow of laughter, "I would venture to say, if there were such thing as a Choir of Worriers, you would be its conductor."

"Yes," Cornelael thundered back jovially, "Oh my, I guess so..."

"Come, walk and update me on other news. I'm bound for the Celestial Hall of Science. I've been informed that newly-arrived scientists will be in attendance. I love their questions and reactions, don't you?"

"You know, dear friend Mason Pringle, that humans are of great curiosity for me," he laughed.

They passed through a gateway hedged with bright-colored hibiscus in full bloom, giving no further thought to the internal disturbance. They made their way, in continuous conversation, down a winding path paved of cobblestone in the color and texture of polished green coral. The City of Knowledge, their destination, shone brightly in the distance.

The godly citizens they passed were in stark contrast to those one may have found on a New York or Chicago street. Imagine taking a stroll in Central Park and encountering people who not only walked, but also floated or flew about you.

A joyful sight indeed to see jovial souls, dressed in multicolored robes, some adorned with sashes and all in some fashion generating affection to one another as they proceeded past. Souls that complemented a picture of vibrant-colored rainbow as its backdrop, augmented by a multitude of pastel-shaded houses with unique designs, set in serene eye view.

Adding to its storybook imagery, it was alive with hordes of magnificent angels: tall ones, short ones, some with armor, others with radiant halos, all joyously intermingled into the heavenly stream. Each had his or her own captivating beauty and auras.

Mason Pringle's friends and colleagues received them as they arrived at the steps of the Hall of Science. Brother Mason was respected there as a Senior Fellow.

They bowed and embraced, magnifying each other's glow as they entered together.

They were part of just one of many groups. Amazingly, for a place that had no accounting for time, everyone arrived together to take their seats in a theater of thousands as the lecture began with precision.

At the podium stood an exquisite Angel with plush wings of pink down, contrasted by a regal gold tunic. She addressed them with vigor in her voice, "Praise is to the Triune God for you, learned souls of science. For the benefit of our new participants, let me introduce myself.

"I am Angel Ancillael. I am a Virtue, created in the first manifestation by the loving will of He who is forever. I lead a Choir of Virtues, with great appreciation and humility." Her tone marked her position of leadership, which everyone recognized immediately. Now that she had everyone's attention, she confidently resumed her orientation.

"As Virtues, we are charged with governance of all nature, and are also known as the 'Spirits of the Elements'. Motion and control are our domain. At times, we are referred to as 'the shining ones', who have control over seasons, stars, moons; even the sun is subject to our command. We are also in charge of miracles, courage, grace, and valor." She raised her arms and flexed her wings, with great fanfare from hovering angels.

"Welcome, heroes of the journey and saints for the love of Him. God enjoys your interest in His science and your zeal for discovering it. Thus, He has provided this forum for those who wish to quench their thirst for further knowledge of Him and His creation."

She proceeded to prepare them by explaining that the questions posed, at times, might very well be answered by other questions back to them. These were to challenge their reasoning. She laughed with roaring gusto and added jokingly, "For all eternity."

The crowd laughed with her.

Then her attention shifted to make a serious announcement--one which offered some explanation as to what they had all experienced of late. She admitted to its existence, and described the phenomenon as a dent in the flow of the Spirit.

She cautioned, "It appears that God is asking us to bear this disruption of the peace with prayer, for the ultimate greater good, and with the assurance that its meaning would eventually unfold to one and all."

Mason Pringle stood to ask a question.

"Yes, Mason Pringle. Glory to God is for you."

"Glorious Angel of God, I am wondering—did the disruption you speak of emanate from the kingdom, or is it planetary?"

"All I can say is that I believe it originates from a human spirit, one residing in a level at Paraclete City. We trust, though, that it serves God's purpose." She waited for a follow-up question, but Mason massaged his beard and sat down.

Then Ancillael knelt with a bowed head, and as she did, the multitude of souls also congregated within the huge crystal auditorium followed her lead. The ceiling opened before them to reveal the presence of an enormous white dove, with softest down and eyes of fire. Its wings extended to the perimeters of the Great Hall.

A golden light surrounded it, one far brighter than that of the largest of suns. Taken with euphoria, those present heard a symphony of angels in song, followed by a resounding, yet gentle and loving voice.

"Dear children of Our issue, We rejoice in your love and are pleased of your will. Here We bestow upon you greater resources to aid in your quest for seeking Us in greater understanding." He followed with a burst of joyful laughter that levitated the assemblage with indescribable joy.

"Remember, as always, the clue to understanding Our science, is that it is <u>One</u>." He laughed again and His presence faded, leaving only the echo of His parting words: "Beloved, We are with you always and forever."

Those in attendance came to their feet feeling a bit tipsy. Ancillael gave praise to God, and posed a series of profound unanswered questions for study: *How did consciousness arise? What is the universe made of? Can the laws of physics be unified?*

Great laughter ensued as the participants contemplated the enormity of the questions posed. They tipped their heads in respect to Ancillael, as if to say *touché*. She smiled with great affection, knowing the depth of their quest. They took their leave to join together in discussion groups, one of which Mason Pringle customarily led.

Cornelael said, "Isn't she something? A sheer bundle of joy, a complete delight."

"She is that and more," replied Mason Pringle.

"When we have our 'Angel Dances', almost everyone wants a dance with her. Even Our Lord, our Merciful Redeemer, cannot resist cutting in. She's also very entertaining, does impressions of humans and other planetary species."

Mason smiled at the mental image. Then he said, "Well, I'm off, dear friend. My study group waits. Praise is to God for you Cornelael, the source of great camaraderie and joy to me."

"Likewise, dear friend Mason Pringle, peace and joy to you."

As Cornelael made off, Ancillael made a surprise visit to Mason, bearing a message. She informed him that God, in appreciation of his capacity for wisdom, requested that he mentor two souls who were shortly to arrive in the realm. Although apprehensive and curious, he did not question God's messenger or His purpose.

Mason extended his hands to her in warm acceptance, and then placed them on his heart.

"I am humbled and graced to serve Him, His Majesty, with my whole being."

Ten

TONY AND ZACHARIAH JOINED Obe at the well, where Obe informed Tony that he would accompany him to visit his family, which Tony heard with some surprise. Preparing him for the journey. Obe warned that it would be difficult for him, but it would be a good opportunity for Tony to enlist prayer and healing.

Obe also reminded him that some of the people they encountered might not be open to his presence, and that they would not see him or hear him in a true sense.

Further, Obe laid the groundwork by stressing that those encounters required Tony's prayerful concentration and that he needed to muster all of his emotional and spiritual energy. In addition, those who were open would be conscious of his presence, making it easier for him to speak to their hearts. In this way, his words would translate to, and be heard by, the personal fashion of their intuition.

Tony, with a heavy heart at the prospect of seeing his grieving family, traveled at light speed toward the earth with Obe at his side. In the blink of an eye, they arrived at the entrance gates of St. Johns Cemetery in Queens, New York.

When Tony saw the red brick administration building, his emotions almost overwhelmed him. He recalled playing outside of this very building while his parents made the purchase of the family gravesite, when the second section was opened in 1933.

"Are we going to my funeral?"

"Yes. The hearse with your remains, followed by family and friends, will be here shortly. I thought you would like to reflect here amongst your departed relatives in preparation."

"Yes, I'd like to. Thank you Obe," he said, nervous and tearful.

In an instant, they were at the edge of a wrought-iron-fenced section, peering in at a large central monument decorated with engraved roses and angel likenesses. Chiseled in bold type at its center was the name

"Romero".

"It's funny," Tony said. "Look. There are the graves of my grandparents, whom I visited often. Their souls are alive in perfection and great happiness. Yet it still saddens me when I think of their deaths. That sense of loss I felt when they died is still so sharp."

"Tony, feelings of love never leave us. They are eternal."

Tony saw an open grave at the left corner, and pointed to it.

"I guess that's where they will plant me."

"That looks like a pretty good place," Obe admitted. "Together with those whom you love and who love you."

Tony detected a twinge of envy in his voice. He turned to Obe.

"You should see where I wound up, in the middle of a cow pasture with a boulder as my head stone," the boy said ruefully.

Sensing the momentary arrival of Tony's body, Obe whispered to him, "They're here," and took Tony's hand in support. Tony braced for an electrical jolt from his companion, but it did not happen.

Obe read his thoughts and smiled. "It's okay; while we are in this realm our chastisement is suspended."

Tony nodded, relieved. Then he gazed back at the proceedings. "Well, there I am, bronze casket and all. Hey, there is our old parish priest, Father Sparachino. Wow—that is something." Tony shook his head in wonderment.

"What a good man. I guess he came out of retirement to say my funeral Mass."

Tony remembered the priest's loving nature. He wished now that he could have spent more time with him. Nevertheless, he was grateful that his wife and kids had remained close to him and his counsel. He recalled the priest's homilies--how he spoke with a hard Brooklyn accent, a cultural stereotype, yet underpinned with substance, intelligence, and earnestness. His words rang with love.

Tony rushed to his family and friends as they exited the funeral cars. He picked up their feelings of grief when they paused under the shade of a maple tree, their faces tearful and solemn. Tony tried to console them with embraces, to let them know how much he loved them. He tried and tried to enlist responses, and grew more and more frustrated.

"I know he's here," his mother whispered to Norma, "I can feel him."

"Yes," Norma agreed, a small, sad smile lifting the corner of her mouth. "I feel him, too."

Norma spoke to Tony with her inner voice.

Tony, why? Tell me, why? I know I busied myself with running the house and did not give you what you needed. But how could you have done that? Cheat on me? And then disappear? If your mother knew, it would kill her too.

Tony embraced her once more, crying, "No! No, Norma, you are the best! You were my best friend. You were a perfect wife, lover, and mother. No other could have given me more."

His sad eyes met Obe's, shame cutting into him. "She's blaming herself." He bowed his head. *My duty was to show her respect and loyalty.*

With welling tears, he whispered to himself and tried to find a reason for his actions again. *I failed in the most important part of life. I wasn't unhappy, so why did I do what I did?*

He shouted as loud as he could, hoping that they would hear. Of course, there was no reaction from the living.

He began to realize how selfish and how caught up in himself he had been. Success in business and the power of money had grown into his sole ambition.

"Please, please, forgive me." His words hung without their acknowledgement, burdened by the realization of his self-interest and thirst for money and power.

His introspection was broken by the voice of the Funeral Director, which also distracted Norma from her thoughts of him.

"Mrs. Romero, please follow me."

The dark-suited, austere-looking man led her and the children to the gravesite, where Tony's casket lay piled high with cut funeral flowers. The others gathered around with forlorn faces awash with tears of grief.

Father Sparachino began the funeral prayers, and Tony positioned himself next to his wife and children. He could pick up the devastated feelings of his parents, who stood next to them.

His father's face was buried on his wife's shoulder. His mother smoothed her husband's hair, sharing the deep loss. A simple working man, Tony's father had admired his son for his accomplishments, as did his mother, a retired seamstress who had pledged every hour of work to her children for their success and happiness. They had loved Tony deeply; and now, just like that, he was gone.

Near the end of the service, the Funeral Director handed out flowers to each mourner as the priest concluded his heartfelt prayers with a final tribute.

"I feel in my heart that Anthony Romero was a true hero, and is, or shortly will be, in the eternal bosom of our Divine Creator. However, we need to pray for his soul and those of the others who have passed, always mindful that God seeks and expects not only good works, but also a close relationship with all of His children. Prayer is the only way that can happen."

After hearing his words, Tony believed that the priest knew of his behavior, and he decided that he didn't want to stay around to find out. He attempted to bolt, but was cautioned by Obe to listen on, to sustain the feelings of shame.

Father asked them to bow their heads for God's blessing, and instructed them to place a flower on the grave as a final farewell to Tony. He made the Sign of the Cross and performed the final blessing... "In the name of the Father, Son and Holy Spirit, Amen."

"Amen," Tony and Obe repeated in soft undertones.

"He eulogized me as if I were someone special." Tony blinked back tears.

"Well, you did give your life for another."

"Anyone would have done the same."

"I'm not so sure about that. I think you have forgotten how self-absorbed contemporary humanity has become."

The solemn-faced Funeral Director prompted Norma to place the first rose on the casket

Tony read her thoughts:

I'm not letting you go so fast. She kept her rage in check, so as not to upset her children. Norma felt abandoned, rejected, and left without a conciliatory attempt from Tony. Questions of guilt played in her thoughts. *Did my harsh words cloud his mind? Did my words distract him from the presence of danger?* Whatever had happened, she was left alone now, to fend for herself and her children.

Her thoughts broke off in order to guide her grieving children in the placement of their flowers. When Tony's parents placed theirs, he felt their broken-heartedness. Choked with emotion and sadness, he tried again to turn away, but Obe stopped him.

"I know this is difficult for you, but it's best if you stay and hear the others."

"You know Obe, what makes this worse for me, is not only that I cannot be with them, but it's the knowledge that I behaved like a beast and took them all for granted when I was with them."

Tony paced in tears, frustrated and angry with himself that he had not expressed the depth of his love for them. He reached out his hands to his family while he continued to pace and weep, and convicted his soul inside. *It was always about me--my needs, hopes, and dreams.*

"Listen," Obe alerted him. "Your sister. Listen to her heart; she's talking to you inside it."

Tony tuned into her internal laments, never thinking that she'd ever stand before his coffin. She remembered seeking shelter in his arms. Her strong older brother and protector, always there when she needed him.

She knew she had been a brat at times but he had always had patience with her. Claire's eyes raised and sought the clouds in prayer, *Father God, I pray that you forgive his failings and bless him with happiness in heaven. Goodbye, my brother—for now.*

Tony's eyes shone. "Obe, my sister Claire is a gem, one of the most patient, loving souls ever, and one of a kind. However, she has it wrong; she is the one who had been there for me. Always my defender, and most of all my motivator. I failed to add happiness to her life."

Tony listened with a somber mind as other family and friends said their farewells. In vain, he tried to embrace the ones that had the most difficulty with his death, especially his business partner.

When most of the mourners had left, a group of strangers came to the site.

"Who are these people?"

"Anthony, these are the souls that fate joined to your destiny. The little girl you saved, with her parents, along with the truck driver and the doorman."

"Oh my God, it *is* them. Their sadness is crushing me inside."

"Listen."

The little girl's father spoke first. "Anthony Romero, we all met at the funeral parlor and felt that we needed to memorialize you in an intimate fashion. We waited until the others left, knowing that our presence would remind them of the cause of their loss. Mr. Barone would like to address you first."

"Anthony, Joe Barone here," the trembling man began. "I believe that I am responsible for your death," he said. He burst into tears as he delivered his emotional burden.

Tony felt the man's deep suffering and his unbearable guilt, chastising himself with the belief that if he had not been yelling at the truck driver, Tony would still be alive. Barone prayed for forgiveness, then, heavy with sorrow for Tony's wife and children he bowed his head, made the sign of the cross, and stepped back, still trembling.

"Mr. Romero, Jimmy Murphy," the burly truck driver, uncomfortable in his suit, said as he stepped forward. He paused, brushed through his reddish hair. His words failed him in his remorse, and he paused while wiping his tears. The others placed their hands upon his shoulders for support as he struggled to speak.

"I... I can't blame Barone here. I'm a professional, never got a ticket and even won awards for driver safety at my company. My day started with a series of mishaps, which caused me to get behind with my stops. The traffic was getting to me. I let everything get to me, and should not have tried to park there."

He removed his cap to wipe his brow and went on, "I also went to church and asked for forgiveness. I'm so sorry.

I wish it had never happened. My wife and I have been praying for your wife and children. They're beautiful."

Jimmy choked with tears and stepped back as the child's parents came forward.

"Anthony Romero, my wife and I," he began to say but stopped, and introduced himself and his spouse with formality.

"Mr. Romero, Cynthia and Arthur Raymon here. We feel we are the blame. We were so excited about the positive things we learned that a movie critic said of my wife's work that we were blindly checking through all the publications. We did not give our daughter proper supervision."

The two of them exchanged glances. "We are stricken with mixed feelings of sorrow, guilt, and gratefulness to you. We pray for your forgiveness. You are a true hero. Thank you."

Tony, moved by their words, embraced each and offered his own forgiveness. He touched the little girl's head and asked God's blessings for her. The little girl felt his presence, and saw part of his image. She tugged at her mother.

"Mommy! Mommy! I see a man. He touched my head...he is smiling!"

"Arthur! Boys... did you hear what our Gloria said?"

They nodded in affirmation, and Jimmy whispered through falling tears, "He heard us. Thank God."

Obe took Tony by the hand, and in an instant, they were in the living room of his Westchester home. It was crowded with mourners, but also with angels, who smiled in welcome at their appearance.

Obe gasped. "Wow, this is a mansion!"

Tony wasn't listening. His eyes were wide at the sight before him. "How could they be here already?"

"Tony, remember...the concept of time."

Tony, excited to be in their presence again, searched for his mother. He found her in the kitchen, preparing food for the guests. She felt his presence as he touched her hand. Then he looked around, wanting to help, as he always did on holidays and special occasions.

"Mom, I am okay. In fact, everything is going to be okay," he said to comfort her.

His mother was able to glimpse Tony's outline. She was startled, yet uplifted at the same time. His words registered in her mind as Norma came in.

"Mom, what are you doing?"

"I thought I'd prepare the salad," she replied.

She took a deep breath. "Norma, I think I'm losing it. I'm sure I just saw Anthony standing here cutting vegetables with me, as he used to do. My mind must be playing tricks, but then I thought I heard his voice inside my head, telling me he's okay. Norma, I believe it's true. He's here."

"I believe you, Mom. I feel him too. I wouldn't put anything past Tony."

"Thanks, Norma. I know Mom and Dad will be in good hands with you," Tony said with sad appreciation, inches from her head.

Obe interjected, "Anthony, it's time for us to move on."

Eleven

TONY AND OBE STOOD before an old country church, its outer walls clad in whitewashed, clapboard pine. Modern-day parishioners were entering this antebellum-era landmark for Sunday service on a lazy summer afternoon. Their number was equally balanced with both black and white worshippers, far different from how it was in the founders' era in 1847, the year of its construction.

At that time, it had served as a place of prayer for prosperous plantation owners and slaveholders, who had abided the preservation of human bondage as a means of economic success–a pursuit assured by righteous ministers, who justified their way of life by the force of their educated rhetoric.

"What are we doing here?" Tony asked.

"I was asked to show you part of my life."

"Who told you to do that?"

Obe hesitated to respond, showing his discomfort at Tony's probing. "The Blessed Spirit within," he said, staring down at his feet.

Tony quickly realized that he was standing in front of the church of Obe's youth. The center, in his time, of his colonial community.

Obe's facial expression had changed.

"This probably brings back nostalgic memories of your childhood and friends," Tony observed.

Obe swallowed hard as he answered him, "Yes. We played here together after Sunday service. We really couldn't wait to see each other, and have a day without work."

It was a tough go for most of those with smaller family farms. The cost of owning slaves was out of their reach, so the farm work fell solely upon them. Obe and his family did not mind that part of poverty. In their eyes, slavery was an abomination.

Obe pointed toward the barn.

"See there, that's where the Negroes ... there behind the barn, they waited, while their masters attended services and the community picnic that followed."

Obe's eyes grew wide as he recounted the joy the slaves had given him. He had enjoyed viewing their own prayer service, and especially loved their soulful singing. Hidden behind a barrel, he had watched and listened to them whenever he could get away.

The slaves had been aware of his presence, but had only recognized him with secret smiles. Sometimes an overseer would chase him away, but not before he had taken the chicken and cornbread that the black servants had inconspicuously left for him atop the barrel.

"You know Tony, I loved their soulful voices and their spirituals. 'The Gospel Train' and 'Swing Low, Sweet Chariot' songs especially. I found out later that they were coded songs that referred to the Underground Railroad, an organization that helped escaped slaves get to freedom."

"I know about the railroad. I studied it in American History class," Tony affirmed. Then he paused and scratched his head; something Obe had said didn't sound right.

"Wait a minute. Underground Railroad? When were you born?"

"I was born April 1, 1848," Obe proudly admitted without hesitation.

"When did you die?" Tony queried, looking confused.

"My soul left the earth on November 23, 1864."

"Wait a minute. So you died at sixteen. Is that right?"

"Yes, or thereabout."

"Hold on here. Are you telling me you have been in Level One for, let me see, this is 2009. You have been here for 145 years?"

"Well, not really. I remained in Level Two for some time before."

"Jesus!" Tony belted in disbelief, and gasped as the ground shook. "Sorry, Lord," he said with an apologetic look to Heaven.

Still trying to take in what Obe had said, he sat down on a bench to bury his head in his hands. Obe joined him, and placed his hand on his shoulder.

"Don't worry. I don't expect you to be there that long. You're a good man, and most of all, you seem to accept God's will."

"This baffles me, Obe. You appeared to have a tremendous love and understanding for God, so what keeps you from Him?"

"This is what everyone asks me. I guess I can only describe it as a 'disagreement'."

"A disagreement? You're telling me you've had a two-hundred-year disagreement with God?" He raised his voice in frustration. "How can anyone have a disagreement with God?"

"That's just it. I do."

"You mean that, even after you have been purged through frightening lower levels, and now for a long period at Level One, you haven't come to terms with yourself? Doesn't that gold strip you have on the sleeve of your robe herald the work you have done in leading souls through the Great Gate?"

"Yes, and I am grateful for the acknowledgement. However, Anthony, scripture tells us to say yes when you mean yes, and no when you mean no, and that if our intentions for God are lukewarm He will spit us out."

Tony stamped his foot. "You know Obe, I have known some crazy people in my day, some certifiable, but you take the cake. You're spiritually crazy, I'd say, for the lack of a better way to coin it."

"Anthony Romero, I'm sorry. Your concern for me, it moves my heart, but we need to go on now."

Within a microsecond, Tony and Obe were in the backyard of a modern-day home in a Fayetteville, North Carolina suburb.

"What are we doing here?" Tony asked, filled with boiled tension.

"There." He pointed into the distance. "There in the woods. Come...see that boulder? That's where my remains lie."

"You mean you're buried here...who buried you?"

"Yes, properly buried by the good graces of my traveling companions. They carried me, wounded and bleeding, next to that rock. The forest stood thicker then, with no homesteads."

"Wounded? Were you in the Civil War?"

"Yes...but no, I wasn't a soldier. I hated the Confederacy; they took my father against his will to fight the Yankees. My father, like me, did not believe in the cause of slavery. A few months after he left, we received word from a neighbor who had made it back home wounded. He brought us the sad news of my father's death. Killed on his first day of battle. Praise is God's for him."

"What happened to you?"

Obe hesitated. "Not long after, my mother and sister died of the fever. I buried them in the church cemetery."

Tony paused with a deep sigh. "Why did we not visit their graves?"

Obe did not answer, but reached his hands out for support and continued his explanation.

Soon after their death, a slave had told him that the Confederacy had arrived in town, and was pressing young boys into service. His brow tightened at the memory, as if, even now, he could see them coming for him, as they had his father. He showed Tony how he had hurriedly gathered as much food and clothes as he could carry and had headed north, making his way through the cover of the forest.

He had hoped to reach New York, where a cousin of his mother lived. He had a letter with an address on it that his mother had received a few years before. This person was his only living family connection.

"Dear God, Obe, what a tragic life. Is this why you are mad at God?"

"Mad at God? Heavens, no! I know that God allows nature to take its course. The other tragedies that befall humanity, like war, are triggered by us, mostly through our affinity for power and money."

Tony, taken with sympathy, just stared at him with sadness.

When they got to the boulder, a shrieking voice greeted them eerily: "Be gone with you! Evil spirits, walk not into my world."

Obe answered, "Elijah Thompson, old friend and caretaker. It is I, Obermyer Coddington."

The ghost of an elderly black man materialized atop the boulder, which startled Tony.

"Retreat, evildoer, for the remains of my beloved friend in certainty lies beneath me. Your trickery is revealed," he cackled.

"No dear friend, look at me. It is I, Obe."

"You too are now in a ghostly state?" the unrested spirit asked with anguish in his voice.

Obe responded with fondness, "No, companion to freedom. I have ascended by the grace of God. I have come to ask you to join your kinfolk in the realm of Heaven. Justice and peace has come to the land where you abide. Look around you; free black men and their families also occupy those dwellings of luxury.

"The calamity you remember does not exist now. Take my hand and look toward the light you have shunned for such a long penitential period. Be not afraid; accept your eternal inheritance."

"Why betray me now, you who have saved the life of my dear child, my precious Paulina?" The specter still could not believe; a lifetime of betrayal had destroyed his trust.

"I do not betray you. Your child, as you would have wished, resides in the celestial kingdom, happy and peaceful, and awaiting you to share her joy."

The ghost came toward them. Mesmerized by the exchange, Tony could only stand and watch.

Suddenly he saw the dark shadow of an ugly winged creature pursuing Elijah's apparition. He stepped back with apprehension, not knowing what to do. He glanced at Obe; he'd seen it too.

All at once a bright light appeared, and in it was an angel, uniformed like a Roman soldier, with a shiny-armored breastplate and sword in hand. Obe addressed Elijah with wonder.

"Praise is to God, he has sent you a protector to lead you to the Kingdom. Be quick, kind friend. Take his hand and be free of your misery."

The dark spirit attempted to pull the old ghost back, but the angel pierced him with his readied sword, causing a burst of fire that consumed the damned spirit, reducing it to ash.

Shaking in fear, Elijah Thompson took the hand of the Angel, who bowed his head in salute to Obe. He did the same to Tony, then carried his charge into the light. Tony stood frozen and speechless at what he had just witnessed.

"'Mad at God'?" Obe declared. "Look at how His Divine Grace pours from His heart of mercy."

Tony, still shaken with emotion, admonished him in a raised voice, "*That* you can accept from God—Elijah's rescue. Well, what about your own?"

Obe stayed quiet.

After a moment of thought, Tony asked, "Will Elijah be joining us at Level One?"

"I don't know, but I am happy that his journey to God can be completed." Obe pointed at the horizon. "We have one more stop to make for you before we return."

Tony was about to question him again, but in an instant found himself on a lounge chair on his partner's patio, next to Albee and his wife, who were both in tears.

Tony fired at Obe, "You have to stop doing that! At least give me a moment to adjust!"

Obe shrugged. "Sorry. I forget you aren't used to such things."

Tony shook his head. He then gazed over to his friends, ears opened to their conversation.

"Maggie, losing Tony and seeing the effect on Norma and the kids convicts me. I know I have been egotistical and selfish. I have shamed you and the kids. My behavior is inexcusable." His voice was heavy, and he had to stop for a moment. He wiped at his cascading tears and went on.

"Tony wanted to go home that night, but I encouraged him to stay and drink. Maybe if he hadn't, he would have been clearer, more careful that morning. I don't know; I just miss him. The business will not be the same without him. He energized me, and always watched out for us."

Albee reached for Maggie with a shaking hand and promised, "From now on I will spend all my free time with you and the kids. I love you. Please forgive me."

His sorrowful words moved Maggie to hug him, but her eyes suggested doubt that he would live up to them.

"Oh, Albee, I know that you have done things, hurtful things."

She went silent and nervously played with her apron, trying to contain her long-held resentment for both him and Tony. With a clenched fist, she inwardly chastised Tony in the great beyond, *I really loved you Tony, but you are both charming bums. What did you think? Screwing around like that. The pain you caused Norma. You drained her of all happiness. I hope God will forgive you, and I pray this will be a wake-up call for Albee.*

Tony heard her and felt a sharp pain in his heart, already weighted with anguish. "I'm sorry," he told her, hoping she'd hear his words. "Yes, Maggie," he affirmed with remorse, "truly a bum. Too many women and too many shots."

Tony sighed with some relief as he read her, and felt the hope she had inside. His passing might have left Albee a gift for a greater appreciation of his family. He saw them now as a couple for the first time.

"Albee, I would like us to go to church as a family again. You have not been to confession and Mass in years. Let's say a prayer for Tony's soul and for strength that we may fortify our life and marriage with good things."

They bowed their heads and prayed the Lord's Prayer. Tony and Obe placed their hands upon them, as the couple's guardian angels appeared, also praying with them. After the prayer, Albee glanced at his wife and their eyes met with a shared calm.

"You know honey, as we prayed, I felt the touch of angels."

"Funny, I did too," she said. She was taken with emotion she peered up towards the sky. "Thanks, Tony. We will pray for you."

Tony felt a stream of energy pass through him at Maggie's words of forgiveness.

"Wow, I would have never believed they felt that deeply about me," Tony marveled, choked with tears once again.

"It's time for our return," Obe whispered with a hand gesture, giving him some warning.

Tony raised his hand. "Wait a minute... wait a minute," he repeated with impatience, "not so fast. You shuffled us out of North Carolina like a thief in the night to hide your denial. As far as I can see, you are just as much a ghost as Elijah Thompson, but stuck in time by your own choosing. And--you saved his child? What was that about?"

"I didn't mean to rush you. Yes, I admit that many feelings flooded into me in that encounter. Maybe you're right; maybe I didn't want to deal with them."

"Well, I know you're not afraid of me..." Tony started as his irritation rose, "...if not afraid of having it out with God. I'm small potatoes. Tell me about the child."

"I will. I'll show it all to you through the Well of Hope when we return."

Twelve

AT THE WELL OF HOPE PORTAL, another soul requested that Obe do an intervention with a soul who had suffered an uncomfortable visit with his own family.

In the meantime, Tony sat on the bench, trying to take in what he had just experienced. He missed his family even more now, but his discomfort and pain was somewhat lighter in intensity than before.

He assumed that the prayers offered for him did in fact have an effect, and supposed that the level of discomfort indicated a soul's proximity to final liberation and his eventual entrance into the Eternal Kingdom.

In a short while, he sensed a presence and opened his eyes. His caretaker, Sister Rose Margaret, stood before him. She had a very thoughtful look on her face.

"Praised is to God for you, Anthony. The Lord God is pleased by your progress, and has sent the highest of His emissaries to meet with you and Obermyer Coddington at the Orientation Level."

Obe appeared through the gray mist, and she informed him of the summons as well.

"What do you think this is about, Obe?" Tony questioned as they followed the Sister to the elevator.

"Well, your guess is as good as mine. They have summoned me from time to time for discussions with Saints and Angels, but only briefly."

"Wow, God has done all that for you and you still resisted?"

"Please, Tony!" he barked with frustration, "It's not resistance, and I wish the feeling didn't exist, but it does."

"I wonder why I have been called. I have only just arrived here."

"That is not unusual. God's ways are not our ways. As you're fond of saying, He holds the cards."

"You say that with some agitation in your voice. I thought you weren't angry at God."

"No, I just get upset when I return from Earth. It leaves me with a strong yearning to join with Him and to see my family."

Obe went on further to offer a philosophical explanation. He touched his heart and described the acute longing he had within him—a feeling of incompleteness at times after he had walked the earth, which he related to an internal detachment to something greater than himself.

Tony nodded in affirmation and offered his own experiences, sharing Obe's anticlimactic feelings. "Yeah, at times in my life, especially when things were going well, I felt a tugging to fill a blank spot. You know, I feel it stronger here to some degree too, Obe."

"I guess it's because we came from God, and I think each of us in an innate way is aware of the separation. So much so, that our inner constitution longs for Him."

Following Sister's lead, they arrived before a pair of tall bronze automatic doors that opened into a large foyer. The space differed in design from the one Tony had visited with Pinchot. The floor was made of marble, with grout lines that brought forth golden light. Fascinated, he brushed his hand over a jeweled mosaic wall, like a child attracted to glitter. The mural depicted Jesus with the Apostles in Biblical scenes.

Sister stopped for a moment to think.

Wow—graduation so soon. But you know best, my Lord. Then, with joy she obediently pointed them to a red velvet bench and exited, with a promise to return with new garments.

Tony, still curious, took the opportunity to question Obe once more as they waited.

"So, Obe, tell me about the girl."

Obe flashed him a "do we have to do this" look, but responded anyway, his words heavy on his soul.

Tony's eyes focused on Obe as he related his story, digesting every word that recreated his journey.

"It took months for me to get to North Carolina. I slept during the day and hiked at night to avoid detection by the Confederate Army. I prayed a lot, and my food seemed to last, as if by some miracle, over the entire journey."

Tony marveled at how his celestial companion had snared rabbits and squirrels to sustain himself, and felt his fear when Obe disclosed the many times he had come close to detection by slave hunters and their dogs.

By his expression, one could surmise the fear he had, yet he had been confident in the backwoods with the training his father had given him. "We'd made many a hike into the wilderness together. I learned to hunt, trap, fish, and select which berries and roots were safe to eat. So I used this knowledge to sustain me, but all along I also felt the hand of God directing me."

Obe paused for a deep breath. Tony, a city dweller, had never been out in the wilds, and was intrigued by his story. Yet Obe hadn't answered him directly, so he questioned him about Elijah Thompson and his daughter once again.

Obe threw him a stare, annoyed by his pressure, but patiently went on with his discourse. His eyes lit up when he told about achieving the milestone of crossing into North Carolina, a journey of many miles, on foot and mostly in the dark. Exhausted, he had stopped to camp, and had placed snares and traps out. He had known to expect the morning heat, so he had wedged himself in a cavern hidden by fallen trees and had succumbed to sleep.

Tony leaned in, mesmerized by his account. Obe told him that he had slept for an extended period, the longest since leaving home. He had awoken at dusk, startled by foraging deer, and had gone down to the creek to drink and to check his traps for game. There he had heard voices, and had peeked through the brush to see members of a Negro family, who were trying to unsnarl a rabbit from his trap.

When he had moved for a clearer view, they had heard him and had scattered into the thick forest. Feeling pangs of hunger, he had collected the snared rabbit and proceeded to check the other traps. Happily for him, each had caught squirrels. He had made haste in skinning and cleaning the game, and then had prepared a small fire to cook his catch.

As the fire smoldered from the dripping fat of meat he had laid back, his mind calculated the balance of his journey. After a short time, he had noticed movement in the woods and heard whispers. He knew the sounds were from the Negroes, who had now come back attracted by the smell of the roasted game.

He had called out to them, "You out there, if you are God-fearing and mean no harm, come and eat with me."

After a period of silence, he had heard a faint response.

"Masser... we are black man."

"I mean no harm to black man or any man. Come and eat."

A tall lanky black man had come out of the woods.

"Sit," he had told him, gesturing to the ground beside the fire. The man, clothed in mended rags, had merely squatted, reluctant to sit. He had nervously glanced about, not knowing whether this was a trap.

Obe had cut off a rabbit leg and handed it to him. The man's eyes had widened, his face conveying dire hunger. But he did not eat; his attention was on the woods. Obe had read his thoughts, and broke the silence.

"Tell them to come too; I have more meat to cook. What is your name?"

The man had hesitated to introduce himself, but his hunger won out.

"I am named Elijah Thompson," he had mumbled, and beckoned with an assuring wave toward the woods. Two women, a young man around Obe's age, and a five-year-old girl emerged and joined them, fear on their faces. Obe had welcomed them with a smile and had encouraged them with reassuring words.

"It's okay. I mean you no harm. Sit and eat."

Eventually they had admitted to Obe that they were runaway slaves, on their way to connect with the Underground Railroad and their eventual freedom in the North.

They had explained that for most of their journey a conductor had guided them, until he had had the misfortune of slipping and breaking his ankle as they crossed a creek bedded with jagged rocks and stones.

Their injured protector had known that his disability allowed him to go no further. He had asked them to carry him to a road where he might gain assistance and not become a detectable burden for them.

Elijah had nodded his head with respect for the man who protected them.

An admirable man, Obe had thought, one who, despite his injuries, counseled the family on how to complete their journey in safety.

The bone-weary slave had motioned to his wife, who produced a quilt from under her apron. Elijah had laid out the cloth before them, and with great excitement had pointed to places in the quilt's design that illustrated a map of disguised locations. This had been a very clever way of directed fleeing slaves to escape routes and assistance; also embedded were coded clues and disguised signs on how to identify safe houses along the way.

"Wow, unbelievable!" Tony interjected. "You experienced history while it happened." Then he caught himself, "That was a dumb way of saying it. Anyway, what about the little girl? And how did you lose your life?"

Obe, with tears welling, continued to impart his story. He told Tony that they had decided to journey together, pooling their skills and resources. His new friends had the map and he had the ability to hunt. After a few days, his companions had relaxed and now trusted him, as did the Negro slaves he had visited behind the church barn on Sundays past.

When they neared Fayetteville, the main road had teemed with Confederate troops and wagons. They had kept themselves hidden in the thick woods to avoid detection. Yet they had remained hopeful, for according to the cloth, a safe house was nearby in a stand of pines.

Although they had anticipated food and safety, they had felt it prudent to wait until nightfall before they ventured further, and had found shelter in the woods behind a big boulder--his eventual gravestone.

The little girl, Paulina, had fallen asleep, but soon after had awoken, startled, from a bad dream. In a daze, she had run into the open field. As fate would have it, at the same time a wagonload of drunken militiamen had been passing through on the main road. They had spotted her, and had fired muskets to frighten her. They laughed as if it were target practice, and prepared to fire again. Elijah started to go for his daughter, but Obe pushed him back and had dashed for her himself.

"I didn't think they would shoot at a white man," he told Tony with a disbelieving shake of his head.

Exhibiting selfless courage, Obe had reached Paulina through a hail of bullets and had shielded her with his body, believing they would stop shooting at the sight of his white skin. The last tragic bullet struck him with mortal accuracy, and his assailants in a liquored stupor made off down the road.

After making sure that the militiamen had gone, Elijah and the others had come to their aid, and had carried them back to the shelter of the boulder. Fortunately, Paulina had not been hurt. Sadly, though, they had witnessed Obe's final moments—the death-rattle of his final breath and the stare of his lifeless eyes.

Tony bowed his head with sadness, and reached his hand out to him. "So you are a hero."

Obe shook his head. "Not a hero. Like you, Anthony Romero, I just did what any God-fearing person would do."

"What happened to the others?"

"When I arrived at Paraclete City and contemplated upon the pedestals, I saw that their continued journey suffered further tragedy."

Obe's vision through the redemptive pool showed him how Elijah and his son Samuel, with reverence, had buried him next to the boulder with their bare hands. They suffered grief over the loss of a kind ally. Even though they were accustomed to injustice, this attack against a white man made no sense to them. However, they had continued journeying onward, consumed by overpowering fear, hunger, and a thirst for freedom.

Elijah had assumed the lead and had taken his brood closer to the village. There, driven by necessity, he had sought out food at a farmhouse, cautioning the others to wait in hiding.

"Forgive me," he whispered as he entered a chicken coop. His presence spooked the birds, and they squawked and scattered as he circled one, intent on its capture. The resultant noise had alerted the farmer who, in his britches, took a shot at him with his long gun from the front porch. Elijah had been hit, but was able to escape with his grip fast on an objecting fowl. Mortally wounded, he still mustered the energy to return to his hungry family. The darkness had hidden his wound from them.

After more running and more concealment, they had stopped in a remote place. His son had made a fire while the women dry-plucked the chicken. Still wary of apprehension, they ate the chicken half-cooked, then snuffed out the fire and rested.

Not long after, Elijah had given out a deep sigh, and they realized that he had perished from the wound he'd concealed from them. Overtaken with great sorrow, they had been unable a cry as they wished, for fear of being detected. They had buried him there in a shallow grave and covered it with stones and branches. After doing so, they had carved a cross into a nearby oak tree to mark his grave, and continued their trek in the darkness.

Elijah's oppression had kept his spirit from following the light. Mad at God for allowing him and his family to suffer brutal incarceration, he had returned to the boulder to search for Obe's spirit and never left.

His son led the others to a safe house. There they were steered through a man-sized drainage tunnel into an underground room and kept hidden for five days. Soon after, their journey ended with them safe and free in Canada, although with the tragic weight of loss upon their hearts.

Tony shook his head again with sadness. "It amazes me what suffering the human spirit has endured over the centuries."

"That's why those who faithfully abide with God's love are called saints and heroes. It's no joke, is it, Tony."

"No joke at all, Obe my friend. Many of us intensify the struggle because we are not in touch with God. Blind to his healing presence. I'm a prime example of that."

Their conversation was interrupted by a blaring sound.

"I hear trumpeting," Obe exclaimed. "They're coming for us now."

The doors opened and Sister Rose Margaret, with a big smile, came out with lively-colored tunics folded over her arm.

"Praise is to God for you both. In you, God is glorified. Dress and prepare yourselves for untold joy and peace," the nun declared with raised eyebrows. She was still bewildered by their unexpected release. "We will proceed to the veranda which overlooks the Fields of Glory to welcome your escorts."

Tony shot Obe an inquisitive look.

"You will soon see why we needed to meet outside," Obe told him with a smile.

Thirteen

TONY AND OBE FOLLOWED THE NUN through golden doors onto a grand terrace, tiled in marble and under an atrium of crystal. It was a serene space, augmented with multi-colored roses that shimmered on trellises around the entire expanse.

Sister Joseph Anthony and Sister Rose Margaret had halos, and wore lustrous colored tunics adorned with breastplates that reflected streams of light. The nuns glowed as they motioned for Tony and Obe to join them. The two inched forward and to their amazement transfigured; they too now imparted saintly appearances, though with less illumination. They beamed with peace, their pain a faint memory.

Obe sang out with joy, "Do you feel it? Praise is to God, Tony. His Divine Mercy has liberated us!" he exclaimed, with a telling quiver of his lip.

"Yes, praise is to God," Tony said, with a breath of joyful relief. "I thought we were in trouble."

"Well, Brother Tony, I still believe I am to some degree," Obe replied. The worried movement of his head revealed the incompleteness of inner peace.

"We'll soon find out."

Obe cocked an ear. "Hey, listen! Do you hear that singing in the distance? Look at the road! Angels are lining up."

"Is Jesus coming?"

"I don't think so; by the sounds of creatures I'm sure it's the Assisian Saint."

Obe was ecstatic, yet he stepped back, showing some remaining reticence. Tony's eyes connected with his, and both knew within themselves that they had unsettled business with God. In fact, their collective misgivings seemed more pronounced, adding to uncertain mixed emotion.

Their thoughts were halted at the sound of horns, which heralded the arrival of a contingency of angels. They positioned themselves on the veranda in military formation.

At the front, their leader, tall and unimaginably handsome, made a truly perfect appearance, his armor glowing like a star. He approached Obe and Tony, who bowed respectfully. The trumpets resounded again and a chorus of angels made a formal proclamation:

"We herald the glorified presence of Michael, Archangel and Saint, Prince and Captain of the Heavenly Hosts, defender against Satan's Principalities and Powers, Rulers of Darkness, and Spirits of Evil in High Places."

Glorious winged creatures gazed upon him with loving admiration and, with outstretched arms, continued their homage, "The Majestic Angel of Light, Leader of Holy Angels, Great Heavenly Physician and Messenger of God, we greet you."

St. Michael reached out his hands toward the assembled group and addressed them in a gentle yet powerful voice. "Children and Saints of God, embodied by the Divine Spirit, Brothers and Sisters of the Divine Son, our Redeemer, and King of Heaven. Eternal Praise and Glory is to Them for you."

They bowed their heads; as he extended his hands and motioned them to rise, the sweet voices of angels sang with joy.

"Give welcome!" Michael announced in a voice that echoed, within the newcomers as well as without.

As they looked on with wonder, a wolf with snow-white fur appeared. He led a procession of diverse animals, all aglow, with a bounce of joy to their step. A jeweled coach followed, pulled by eight white horses with plumes of gold.

In it was the person of St. Francis, haloed, with a princely crown upon his head and adorned in a silk robe of vibrant blue belted with a golden rope. Francis beamed a smile of great affection as Michael continued his introduction.

"Hark, he arrives, the Great Humble Servant of God and His Divine Son."

"Praise is to God for you, Devoted Angelic Patriarch of the Heavenly Realms," Francis exclaimed as he disembarked. There were two pure-white doves upon his shoulders. Michael joined the Saint at his side as Francis waved to those assembled. They in turn bowed reverently as he spoke.

"Eternal peace and joy is awarded by the Prince of Peace to you, Obermyer Coddington, and you, Anthony Romero who, like Our Lord, were martyrs for humanity."

Hearing this, Obe and Tony knelt, as did those assembled.

"No, no... rise. We are eternal brothers," Francis insisted, encircling the two with a humble embrace. Then he touched some of the others around him, which caused them to glow even more.

He turned to the new members. "Come now, journey with me through the Great Gates into the Eternal City of God."

A bedazzled Obe and Tony glanced back in disbelief at the nuns and their applauding guardians, and followed Francis into the coach. Francis petted the doves nestled upon his lap as he spoke them.

"You will be greeted by generations of your families. After a time, I will accompany you to the dwelling of our Brother Mason Pringle, who will guide you in the heavenly realm."

Obe's mind questioned, *Why are we not to have own abodes, or reside with their families?*

Reading his mind, the Saint provided an answer.

"You will have access to your families and friends as much as you wish, in fact to the most of heaven, with the exception of the Throne for now. Brother Obe, the question that remains between you and God must conclude," he chided with raised eyebrows. "Brother Anthony will remain with you, as you both progress through the fulfillment of God's plan."

Tony was overwhelmed by it all. He smiled, but his face reflected disbelief. *How can I be worthy of this?* he asked himself.

The coach traveled through a shimmering lush valley, and before long they were able to see in the distance a sparkling city, elevated in the air and bedded upon a cushion of cotton-candy-like clouds.

They came upon a bridge made of exquisite marble, supported by statues in the likenesses of the Holy Family with attending angels. It spanned what look liked a deep, bottomless abyss, over to what one could assume was an island.

On the other side were two enormous mother-of-pearl gates. The tops protruded through a shiny mist, guarded on each side by countless angels singing songs of praise.

"My God," Tony said with awe, and added in a reverent whisper, "The Gates of Heaven. It's amazing; you can feel the profound love of God and a sense of permanence, like they have been anchored here forever."

They passed between the opened portals and halted. The newly-arrived men were struck speechless at the sight of the extraordinary beauty before them. They not only saw, but also felt it in every particle of their being. Everything in perfect order and balance, dressed in colors that spoke to the essence of the Creator.

Francis raised his arms and with deep admiration for God said, "This is our inheritance, as Our Lord promised us."

Tony nearly burst with elation. "No one...I tell you, no one...on earth can ever imagine what we see before us. Every fiber is electrified. This cannot be described...a perfect peace encased in beauty that is impossible to understand or explain...it just must be experienced," he said, with a glance at Obe.

"If this doesn't do it for you, then you're doomed," he added.

Obe blinked, but remained silent.

The coach came to a stop before two lavish floral gardens. Their respective beatified relatives were waiting in front of each. Overjoyed, they exchanged surges of energy and escorted the new arrivals into their individual family reunions. There, family members who came from countless generations and cultures greeted them.

In an instant, they became aware of both their ancestral histories and the uniqueness of their descendants. Francis's mystical presence joined each party at the same time, enjoying each festivity equally in both locations.

After a time the angels escorted them back to the coach, where Francis awaited. The coach then proceeded to their new dwellings, and to those who awaited them.

Fourteen

MASON PRINGLE'S ABODE, a simple lime-colored adobe-style dwelling, sat back in a peaceful setting, against the backdrop of a multi-colored horizon. Mason and his friend Archangel Cornelael awaited the arrivals at a floral trellis out front. Varieties of animals were also present; all anticipated the arrival of the famous Saint and his charges.

"Praise and Glory is to God for you, Divine-favored Saint," Pringle exclaimed with a respectful bow to Francis. Cornelael also bowed with quiet joy.

Francis stepped down, followed by Obe and Tony, and offered a return greeting.

"And praise to Our Lord is for you, great soul of love and humility, and to your royal companion Cornelael, Defender of the Throne." He embraced them, exuding violet-colored sparks of his energy. Then, smiling, he turned and introduced them to Obe and Tony.

"The Lord our God has entrusted you to the most worthy of His children - Mason Pringle, renowned professor of physical sciences and biblical scholarship."

"Welcome to my dwelling, and praise is to God for you, brothers Obermyer and Anthony. I am honored by your presence, martyrs both for children of God."

Francis released his charges to Mason, along with more energized embraces, and re-boarded his coach, where animals sat waiting to revere him. He waved with joy to the admiring souls who had also assembled, and the coach departed down the illuminated path.

Tony, curious, whispered to his friend, "Brother Obe, tell me why we should be so honored to have a grand saint like Francis accompany us?"

"I have had the same thought. Maybe the clue lies in what he represents--a tireless itinerant preacher with a sense of urgency to bring the Gospel message to all God's creatures. How that applies to you or me is not clear."

After their final wave to the saint, Mason Pringle smiled at them and said, "I have prepared refreshments; sweet tea for Obe and Italian espresso for Anthony."

They entered into a modest foyer and passed through to a large living room with pastel-colored couches of shimmering silk. Alongside them were granite-topped side tables. The center coffee table, decorated with flowers, floated above the luxurious marble floor. Atop were platters of pastries.

"Please make yourselves comfortable, and allow yourselves a time of meditation. You know, to catch your breath, as they say on earth. Later I will show you your quarters, and if you like, we can all go to the stadium to see the Sky-Ball match."

"It is a game of high excitement, something like football, but with greater dimension," Cornelael added with excitement.

"Come, Cornelael, let us take our leave while they rest in reflection."

The two progressed down a long hallway, which opened to a garden atrium.

There Cornelael shared his concern. "Mason Pringle, did you feel it? It started for me as the coach approached the house. The feeling became stronger."

"Yes, I did too, even more so in the house."

"Why, may I ask, are they to dwell with you?"

Before he could answer, an Archangel materialized before them. "Praise and Glory is to God for you, Mason Pringle, and you, my brother Cornelael."

"Praise is to God for you also, beloved brother Columbael," they responded, surprised looks upon their faces.

"Professor, The Most High has sent roses, a token of His love from the Throne Garden. Seek insight in them for your divine task. He is pleased with your faithful service and in your guidance of His newly-emancipated children."

Columbael handed him two perfect white roses with the sweetest, most unimaginable fragrance. Mason gracefully accepted them, and dropped to his knees in a quiet prayer of thanksgiving. When he arose, he noticed that one of the extraordinary roses had a pronounced red spot, like a drop of blood, upon it. He was about to speak, when Columbael embraced them both with a thunderous burst of energy. In an instant, he de-materialized, leaving Mason and Cornelael without an explanation as to the spot.

Mason shrugged his shoulders. "I will place these glorious roses in the vase at the center of the atrium. The aroma is filling me with such joy that I can't think."

"It is quite euphoric. My feathers are tingling," Cornelael said. Then he fingered the rose and asked, "Mason Pringle, what do you suppose that red spot represents?"

"I have no idea, but it is intriguing, isn't it? Come, let us complete our tasks."

Fifteen

TONY, OBE, I THOUGHT WE'D TAKE a leisurely coach ride to the Great Stadium of the Universe, through the extra-terrestrial jungle," Pringle suggested.

Cornelael nodded in agreement. "Yes. Oh yes, it is so beautiful there."

Tony and Obe smiled their approval, and they made plans to leave.

Waiting for them outside was a magnificent coach, which resembled what some might call a winter sled, snow-white and gilded in gold. Its seats were appointed with tufted leather-like material, and softer then sheepskin.

In awe and wonder, Obe and Tony mounted the coach, with Pringle and Cornelael behind them.

As the coach began to move, Tony noticed something odd. Startled, he cried, "Where's the driver?"

Mason answered with a smile, "I'm driving. You can too if you wish," he added with a chuckle. Tony and Obe's eyes widened at the wonder of it all.

In what seemed like a second, they were at the edge of a forest blanketed with a canopy of spectacular trees and foliage. Some of them had enormous leaves as big as bed sheets. Each plant had a unique color and texture, and they emanated subtle sounds that drifted out in harmonious tones. Some spoke, while others sang beautiful, lyrical songs to them as they passed through.

After a short distance, Mason stopped the coach at a pool of sparkling water, fed by a cascading tropical waterfall and bordered by a stand of spellbinding coconut palm trees. They sat under them on benches of petrified wood, which overlooked the bright turquoise body of dancing water.

Cornelael touched a palm tree, outstretched his hands, and a large coconut fell into them. He touched the tree in this manner repeatedly, with the wonder of a child, until he had one for each of them.

Mason took his and inserted his index finger with ease. Obe and Tony marveled as their mentor sipped from the hole. Taking his lead, they enthusiastically followed suit.

"Oh my!" Obe cried out. "An extraordinary essence! One that thrills to the core!" He sipped again, rolled the liquid around in his mouth, and swallowed. "You are soothed by its texture, as you taste its sweet flavor. Hard to describe--it's as if every droplet radiates pleasure through your entire body. Try it, Tony."

Tony punctured his easily and shook his head, once again taken with the wonders of this realm. "On earth I needed to puncture the coconuts with a nail and hammer." He took a sip, and as he did, his face lit up. "You know, you're right! Like everything else here, there's no vocabulary that can truly describe anything. Everything speaks to God's greatness."

There was a movement close by, and Pringle turned his attention to it. He smiled. "Look, Cornelael! Arranae and his son Arrantee approach." He raised his voice to call to them. "Praise is to God for you, my brothers."

They stood to greet the two.

"And to you, dear scholar of God, Mason Pringle." Arranae smiled at everyone in turn. "Arrantee and I decided to spin today. The newcomers seem to enjoy the designs."

The two were dressed in velvety, earth-colored, high-luster tunics. Tony and Obe tingled at their affectionate contact.

"Praise is to God for you. Welcome to Paradise."

Arrantee pulled at his father's tunic and whispered in his ear, "Did you feel it when you touched the young one?"

"Yes, I did, but... shush..." he whispered back.

Arrantee separated from the group and sat on a distant bench as the others continued to converse, making suggestions as to which plants and trees to see in the forest.

Tony's gaze wandered, then zoomed in on Arrantee. In a fright at what he saw, he gripped Obe's tunic. Following Tony's eye, Obe stepped back in amazement.

Arrantee had transformed into an eight-foot spider-like creature, with six arms and the mouth and face of a fearsome tarantula.

Arranae noticed their discomfort and glanced back at his son. "Arrantee, please," he chastised impatiently.

The young man transformed back.

"Please forgive him. My son has a propensity for baroque comedy."

Mason and Cornelael laughed with great gusto, and the now-relieved Tony and Obe joined them.

"You see," Arranae said, clarifying what they had just witnessed, "we are not of humanoid nature."

Mason explained that they came from the planet Ara, a planet currently undetected by the Earth's astronomers. "It is situated within the Alpha-Centauri star system and housed in the constellation of Centaurus—a neighbor to Earth in the realm of things; actually the closest star system to the Earth's solar system."

Tony and Obe began to understand the depth of Mason's education as he elucidated further about the nature of the Ara culture. He explained that Ara's inhabitants might look like a species of Earth-bound spiders, but they were very dissimilar. Their internal organs were very much like those of humans.

He flashed a warm smile to Arranae. "However, their brains are more highly developed, which allows them more capability in the field of advanced sciences."

Arranae, with a proud expression, offered a perspective on their biology. "Yes, we have spider-like legs; however, we also have fingers attached to them—in actuality, six sets of five, which give us great advantage in manufacturing and technology design. Our anatomy has qualities that give us greater physical ability; for example, our musical instruments have many more functions and features to promote melodious sound. Some of which can produce a short symphony in themselves.

"We also have the ability to weave silk artistically. In fact, my son and I just completed a new design before you arrived. Cornelael, would you like to show it to them? You know the location—the tree line just to the right of the field of flowers."

"Oh yes, it will be delightful to see." Cornelael beckoned Tony and Obe to follow him. They waved goodbye to Arrantee, who mischievously transformed again, waving back with his three right legs.

"Please..." Arranae said, admonished him once again, "pay him no mind."

"Cornelael?" Obe asked as they walked.

"Yes?"

"I'm curious; does Arrantee's species have souls, as we do?"

"Oh, yes, very much so. The only difference is in the sense that their will has been in strict harmony with that of God's since the time of their creation. Unlike that of yours."

Obe's question sparked Tony to speculate, *Wow! Beings exist that have a nature different from our own. Some of which are in total communion with God, lacking the struggle of asserting free will.*

"They have no beef with God," Cornelael said jokingly, in a fair impression of New York street vernacular. They all laughed, and with a loud chuckle he added, "You will come to know that, in fact, there are many species you will encounter in the realm that have been similarly formed."

Tony added, "I'd like to be there when the NASA astronauts reach Ara. I think the scientists will pack up their telescopes and microscopes and call it a day."

They arrived at a clearing and were stunned to see a four-story tapestry of web, a creation of indescribable lifelike beauty, intricately spun with the likeness of the Virgin Mother holding the infant Jesus.

Back at the pool of water, Arranae questioned Mason. "My friend, please forgive this intrusion of thought but...have you experienced a...certain... unrest... for the lack of a better word?"

"Yes, Arranae, you are not alone. Many of us now, if not all of us, feel it too. We have been told that it is all part of God's plan, that there is no breach of His Divine and Sacred Promise of undisturbed eternal peace, and that we must allow it to unfold."

"Yes, of course it is not for us to question. Curiously, though, it seemed to be somewhat stronger in intensity when you introduced us to Tony and Obe. Especially Obe. It unnerved Arrantee. That's why he moved away and sat on the bench."

"Yes, I have felt that too. Again, let it unfold. Praise is to God for you, Arrantee of Ara. We must move on to the Stadium for the opening ceremony of the Sky Ball game."

Sixteen

THE STADIUM OF THE UNIVERSE bustled with the arrival of heavenly citizens, both on foot and in fairy-tale-like carriages of all kinds. Some were self-powered, while others were drawn by an assortment of animals, horses, unicorns, and a myriad of unidentifiable exotic creatures.

The enormous U-shaped stadium had six tiers of plush seating. The arriving attendees entered via long, automated ramps that conveyed them on a cloud of silvery mist. Sparks of energy were everywhere as the souls greeted each other with cordial embraces.

The four of them sat in a box at the crest of the U-shaped arena and felt the great joy and excitement of those present.

Horns sounded over the voices of the crowd, who immediately quieted down. Choirs of angels, who sat in blocks of hundreds, began to sing team anthems, with each section sporting tunics in team colors.

The singing became more intense as the two opposing angel teams entered the field and took positions on each side of the center dividing line.

The field appeared in some fashion like that of a football field. There were iridescent yard lines without numbers that were spaced evenly down the length of the field, covering a distance of at least twice the length of a customary football field.

An assortment of barber-pole-type goals stood at the corners and midfield. In addition, there were twelve golden rings, spaced at intervals and floating above in a circular movement, a dance which captivated the eye.

Above the crowd, an enormous angel dressed in a sparkling rainbow-colored referee's tunic appeared and flew toward the center, carrying a large silver ball. As he descended, his wings extended and hovered over the starting circle. All eyes were on him as he began to address the crowd.

"Praise is to God for all of you. By the grace of Him, I am the Archangel Miranael. Let us pause now to embrace the Triune God in thanksgiving for our eternal joy."

As they bowed their heads, a vibrant red-colored wind whirled around the stadium and softly caressed the cheeks of all in attendance, causing them to fill with joy.

To everyone's surprise, Jesus manifested Himself next to the Archangel. All went automatically to their knees with gasps at His beauty.

"Why did we fall to our knees?" Obe asked.

Tony answered, "Don't you see him?"

"See who?"

"You don't see him? It's Jesus."

"Where?"

"Standing there, next to the Archangel. Wait, He is speaking."

"My beloved, glory is to the Father, the SonH and the Divine Spirit for you. Please take your seats."

After everyone had gotten re-settled, Jesus grinned at them and said, "You know, I asked the captains of each team if they would allow Me to play, and they rejected Me."

The crowd roared with laughter.

"Yes, they suggested that I'd take unfair advantage," He said, prompting more resounding laughter. "So then, I asked if I could sing an anthem, and you know what? They actually laughed!"

The crowd roared once more.

"Not giving up, I also asked if I might dance, and did not receive an answer. Just kind of a blind stare. So, I took it as encouragement." The crowd bellowed heartily again.

Jesus looked through the crowd. "Ancillael, my daughter," He called, "Please join me in a dance."

Archangel Ancillael laughed and blushed as she flew down from the bleachers and ceremoniously curtsied before Him.

"My Lord, how can I refuse?" she said, with a sweep of her arm and a curtsey.

The music began, sweet and rhythmic, lifting all from their seats in one motion. An enormous band, with members comprised of human and non-human creatures, began to play musical instruments of enormous complexity.

Jesus and Ancillael, at center field started an upbeat circle dance with smiles and laughter, a movement reminiscent of the Hebrew *hora*, the Italian *tarantella*, or the Greek *sirtos*.

Members of the crowd, taken with euphoria, joined them as they broke into the largest-ever line dance.

Obe was still at a loss. He squinted and peered, looking all around the crowd that had gathered on the field.

"You can't see Him? He's magnificent! Words cannot describe His beauty. His features are a conglomeration of every race, with the best elements of each. Simply breathtaking."

"No, Tony I don't see Him, but I feel Him, and am filled with joy and gaiety."

Mason Pringle glanced over at Cornelael and prayed a silent prayer: *Dear and wondrous Master, this is puzzling. All of your creatures share equally and are loved by you equally...*

God's voice thundered inside him: *My loving son, does your trust in Me wane? You know that the eyes of a soul do not open with reason but with the example of love. Continue to be that example.*

Mason prayed with anguish, *Oh yes, Divine Creator. Forgive my troubled thought, which is in itself a puzzlement.*

Cornelael, as if privileged to hear Mason's internal discourse with God, reminded him, "We must let it unfurl." Cornelael winked, and intense euphoria took hold of them both as their attention re-focused upon the dancing multitude.

The dance ended with everyone in the chain. They embraced each other, causing explosive flashes of golden light and sounds that caused all to glow. At once, the angel teams took to the field and headed toward Jesus, whom they embraced with delight.

Jesus ascended, waving to all, and disappeared.

The team captains then stationed themselves at the center. With the referee watching over the proceedings, they readied themselves for the beginning of the game.

Archangel Miranael dropped the silver ball. It descended slowly, and stopped at eye-level of the waiting players. The opposing captains looked across at each other and readied themselves by extending their arms and wings.

The referee shouted, "Let us begin!" and dropped the ball between them. They jostled for it with all their extremities--wings, arms, legs, and heads. Somehow, to the delight of the fans, they managed to entangle the referee between them. Finally, one of them found a way to pass the ball to his teammate, which brought forth cheers from the crowd.

"It's amazing!" Tony shouted with wonder at their agility. "They fly, walk on air, do somersaults, and laugh all the way. Mason, what is the object of the game?"

"Oh, Brother Tony, that's just it, there really isn't any. See out there? The golden hoops at every corner and in the center high above the stadium downfield, which we can presume are the goal posts?

"The object is to get the ball through them. However, there is no point system, really, and no real winner or loser. Just the joy of playing and the comic antics of the angels."

"My goodness, did you see those flips that that blue angel just did? It's remarkable how swift they are with those large wings! Wow!" Obe said, filled with excitement.

The game continued on this way, with more daredevil moves and aerial acrobatics, and eventually ended with the participants and spectators dancing together about the field.

After the celebration, Mason suggested that they attend a symposium at the Center of Spirituality, where a renowned mythologist, Mortimer Thomas, was to speak.

Mason asked their choice of transportation. "Should we call for a coach, transport by instant re-location, or take a leisurely walk?"

Tony deferred to Obe.

"I think a leisurely walk would give me the opportunity to meditate."

"You should," Tony said, a hint of frustration in his voice. "There is no reason why you were not able to see the Lord. You block yourself from Him with your stubbornness."

Obe just glanced at Tony with a tense curl of his lip, and they began their walk to the Center.

Divergent species of blossoming trees and flora edged the road on which they traveled. The scent of flowers permeated the air. One not only inhaled the aroma, but also felt the aura of their velvety texture.

Tony and Obe were amazed by the multiple levels of sensation. What was even more astonishing was the discovery that, if they pondered any one particular genus, it talked internally to them and glorified God by recounting the history of its creation.

PART TWO

Seventeen

THE CENTER FOR SPIRITUALITY sat at the end of a winding road, surrounded by pools of sparkling water with luxuriant multicolored fountains and statuary in the likenesses of aquatic creatures. As they entered the shell-shaped domain, an even greater sense of peace and well-being took hold within them.

"Wow!" Tony said, "This is extraordinary. I am running out of vocabulary to describe things here. Everything is astounding." He grinned as he gazed around him. "Boy, my kids would love it here. I can visualize them jumping with excitement."

"It is remarkable," Obe agreed. "And there... look at those tall, pink-plumed birds! Their vibrancy radiates out to you."

"Those," Cornelael explained, "are called 'Birds of God's Passion'. They are only found here in the celestial realm. Although most of them inhabit Throne City and other places of sacred spirituality, some of them have chosen to come here. See how they nestle together, with great love for each other."

As they approached the gateway into the Center itself, Mason advised them, "This is a place of great sensitivity. It is very serene and calm, and eyes may turn our way as we enter. Perhaps even more so than when we entered the stadium."

"Yeah, I wanted to ask you. What's that about?" Tony asked quizzically.

Obe promptly interjected, "I believe it is I who carry the unrest that the souls are experiencing." There was a flicker of shame in his eyes.

"You... you think it's you?" Tony asked incredulously.

"Why?"

Mason interrupted with a cautionary word, "Let it unfold. Leave it for now, and let us enjoy the great speaker we are about to hear."

The entryway opened into a vast garden formed into the shape of an amphitheater, where people sat on different tiers that overhung a center island. On it stood an enormous white olive tree. Its grand trunk held smooth ceramic-branches, upon which was an abundance of beautiful leaves.

Cornelael nudged Mason. "Mason Pringle, they are looking, as you predicted."

Pringle nodded knowingly, and pointed to some empty seats. "There...let's sit there, near the tree."

As they did, they heard a loud gasp from someone in the crowd around them.

"Look!" he called, pointing. "The tree! A leaf is stained red!"

Others looked to where he was pointing, and also gasped at the sight of it.

"Mason Pringle, beloved friend, the leaf has the same red spot as the flowers the Most High gave you," Cornelael said with unease.

"Yes, indeed it has," Mason confirmed with a knowing tilt of his head, his expression one of sheer calm. He pointed to the entry. "I see the Angel Host and the speaker descending; let us focus our attention."

Tony's and Obe's interest in the tree was quickly eclipsed by the strange figure before the crowd.

"Peace and Joy to you, exalted children of God. Welcome to those of you who have recently arrived. I am Sepulael, an angel of God's Cherubim Choirs. We Cherubs are the protectors of the Most High's Throne. I know that my appearance may be somewhat confusing to some of the new arrivals: four wings to hands... and hooves," she began. "But I dare you to race me..." she joked, flapping her wings.

The crowd roared with laughter.

Once the noise died down, she continued. "The Center for Spirituality is a school of sorts, which guides souls if they wish to further spiritual exploration. He, our Almighty Creator, the Great I Am, Who is profoundly Spirit with material aspects, beckons us all to a deeper closeness here. This is attainable through the gift of our free will, His ultimate gift of infinite love bestowed equally upon each and every one of us."

A cloud of blinding light suddenly encased the tree and Jesus appeared in its midst, causing all to fall automatically to their knees.

"Dear children of Our issue," He started with a beatific smile, "praise and glory is to Us for you. The splendor you find yourselves in comes from the depth of Our eternal love, because of the sacrifice you made for communion with Us. Know that you are cherished here in Our Triune realm.

"The spiritual journey you continue to make will have no obstacles, no interference by dark creatures. Every step you take to seek knowledge of Us will give you greater joy."

Jesus lifted His arms, and a red wind blew gently over those present, leaving them euphoric, as it had at the stadium. They levitated from joy as He took His leave.

After what seemed a millennium of indescribable bliss, they heard the voice of Angel Sepulael, faintly at first. In moments, everyone assumed their prior state.

"Did you see Him this time, Obe?" Tony whispered.

"No, but like before I felt the joy of His presence."

Tony shook his head and looked sternly at his friend.

Obe blew out a short, exasperated breath. He gestured impatiently toward the speaker. "Let's listen, Tony, okay? Leave off with the questions."

Sepulael began, a hand over her heart. "Okay, beloved children of God, it is with great pleasure that I introduce our brother Mortimer Thomas, who spent the better part of his earthly life trying to discover the essence of God."

Sepulael clapped her hands and fanned her four wings as the speaker took his place at the podium.

Mortimer, a burly but gentle man, bowed and raised his hands high. "Greetings. Praise is to God for you, my brothers and sisters. In my career as an anthropologist on Earth, my work focused upon explaining and reconciling what humanity called the 'great myths' of the world's religions."

Mortimer told them that, as a psychologist in his earthly life, Carl Jung's theory of the 'collective unconscious' had influenced him deeply. He had accepted Jung's theory that proposed that this was the inherited part of the human psyche, not one that was developed from personal experience.

Tony whispered to Mason, "This is going to be deep." Mason gestured, a little impatiently, for him to be quiet.

"Using this theory of collective unconscious as my foundation, I developed the hypothesis that myths, ritual practices, and folk traditions were shared in certain symbolic religious themes and patterns of behavior."

He explained that he had studied myths from many cultures: ancient Greeks, Hindus, Buddhists, Mayans, Norse and Arthurian legends, Native Americans, and the Bible, to elucidate their commonality in order to justify his lack of faith in a personal God.

"Yes," he said, "I did find many commonalities, of course, because the souls of all men emanate from our Creator and the thirst for Him is equally present in all of creation."

Obe scratched his head, not knowing where the scientist was going with all this. Tony's eyes met his in agreement.

"But through Divine Revelation," he admitted, "I realized that I had misused Dr. Jung's theory to support my own egotistical will, which I would not allow to be subordinate to that of God's."

Obe refocused when he heard the word "will" used. *Now I get it. It's me again.*

"I came to see," Mortimer explained, "that my reluctance to believe in a personal God existed because, in doing so, I'd be required to adhere to God's expectations. I'd have had to accept the reality of sin, leading me to a requisite of personal sacrifice that I was unwilling to endure."

Upon hearing, this, Tony peered at Obe, who had buried his head into his hands, apparently touched by Mortimer's words.

"In my blind reason, I had packaged God into a less intrusive concept, one which relegated Him to a cosmic energy, one that permeated through all living things. In essence, a collective God-force without accountability."

He further elucidated that his earthly wisdom, education, and life experiences were based upon what he had chosen to believe. "It was a concept disguised and alleged by rational scientific thought, leaving me spiritually bankrupt," he said.

The crowd reflected their approval as he concluded, "I had the opportunity to explore my doubts about God, as many souls do in their search for faith. Nevertheless, I confess that I did not search for faith, for God, in an intimate personal sense. Instead, I searched for ways to fortify my own ego and sense of personal power. Thusly, I misused my many God-given gifts, and consequentially misled many souls to be distracted from Him, and from His perfect love, peace, and mercy."

As Professor Thomas finished, Obe lifted his head and stared at him with a forlorn and confused expression.

A hand came up from a woman in the audience.

"Praise is to God for you, Dr. Thomas. Your words have been stirring. But don't you think, just by the fact that we are all here in the wonderment of Heaven, that in a way you're preaching to the choir? Please excuse the pun..."

The audience burst into laughter.

Mortimer grinned. "Oh yes, thank you, you're absolutely correct. One would believe there is no need. In fact, my original discussion plan covered what I had learned on a recent visit to the planet Ara, and to share the experience of joy I felt from their faithful culture."

His remarks caused the Aras present to transfigure into their cultural form and applaud loudly with their many furry arms.

"Thank you, thank you. I believe, though, that the Holy Spirit guided my words. It may be because of the imbalance we have collectively felt of late."

He bowed to the audience with humble appreciation, praising the Triune God for them, as Angel Sepulael thanked him and took the center, applauding with her many wings.

"Okay now, here is the meditation question for you--one which will no doubt provide challenges and create a wonderful discourse for when we next convene."

She unrolled a golden scroll and read from it. "*Did God's infinite patience and indulgence for the human culture on Earth, and others throughout His Universe, go to such lengths to protect free will that He would allow them to destroy themselves through the use of weapons of mass destruction?*"

Tony, Obe, and the others took leave of their seats. The 'lingerings' of the participants as they left echoed everywhere, as everyone enthusiastically listened to chosen replayed passages of Mortimer's words.

"I know it's because of me," Obe told Tony.

"What? The question? Or what the speaker said?"

"I guess both. I don't know what it means. The leaves turning red when we entered—was it because of me? But I do know that his talk had to do with me."

Tony sighed irritably. It was all he could do to keep from agreeing with him, and loudly. "For now, just meditate on Dr. Thomas' words. He has much more intelligence than both of us put together."

He calmed his words when he saw Obe getting more agitated. "We all went through periods where we thought we should have had greater status. I guess that is part of the process, learning to control our will and learning to accept the 'Big One'. Right?"

Mason joined in on the conversation. "As far as those leaves are concerned, I'm not sure what the red spots mean. The only thing that comes to mind is those occasions on Earth when statues of Our Lord and those of His Glorious Mother dripped blood, as a sign of sadness due to sin or humanity's disconnection from God."

"Is that what it is? Blood?" Obe looked despondent. "I am truly a blight on the souls of heaven," he lamented.

Cornelael lifted him up with his wings, bringing him eye-level, and gazed deeply into his eyes. "Precious son of the Father, brother of the Great Redeemer. He who Is defines the word 'mercy'. Seek Him deeply, Brother Obe, and be at peace."

Obe's eyes welled up with tears.

"Okay Cornelael, put him down now. Let us be off to the pomegranate harvest. Our next stop will lift his spirits," Mason insisted, as a coach instantly appeared.

Eighteen

THE COACH SWIFTLY TRANSPORTED them to a great stand of pomegranate trees. As they disembarked, Tony looked around at the foliage with a wry smile.

"As I remember, Mason, these things were difficult to eat... Lots of seeds, but the surrounding juice sacs are delicious. My father called them Chinese apples."

"Well, remember where you are Tony. I'm sure you will be pleasantly surprised," Mason chuckled. "Look, the angels are calling us to sit there in the clearing."

Cries of great joyfulness greeted them, and they seated themselves at a table loaded with large bowls of freshly-harvested pomegranates. Also before them were pitchers of juice and crystal glasses.

Cornelael poured for the four of them.

Obe was the first to take a sip. "The taste is amazing! Actually, Tony, there are many different flavors all at the same time. Refreshing."

"Yeah, how is this possible?" Tony agreed after tasting his own.

Cornelael and Mason laughed heartedly.

"Cornelael, my brother, I guess we have a couple of souls here who have difficulty with the unexpected. I can't wait to see their reaction when they taste the wine from Our Lord's vineyard," Mason said with a belly laugh.

Mason was pouring more juice, when a young woman with stunning simple beauty approached and tapped Obe on his shoulder. Her touch caused a jolt of joyful energy to flash through him. The glass fell from his hand when he saw her.

"Praise is to the Most High for you, Obermyer Coddington."

He was speechless for a moment, but finally found his voice. "And, also to you, sister. Do I know you? I mean, do you know me?" His words stumbled out, off balance, causing silent amusement among his friends.

"Oh, yes. You kissed me once, in the earthly realm."

Obe blushed. "I did?"

"Remember the apple orchard?"

Tony snickered as Obe blushed as red as the pomegranates before him.

The young woman turned to greet the others with a smile. "Praise to God for you, fellow residents of Paradise."

They answered in kind, their expressions both eager and curious. Obe scratched his head, trying to remember her.

She smiled at his obvious bemusement. "Brother Obe, maybe you will remember me this way."

In a flash, she transfigured into a fourteen-year-old black slave girl in colonial dress.

Obe cried out in joyful surprise. "Abigail Farley! It's you! Praise to the saints in heaven, it is really you!"

Abigail smiled and took his hand, delivering another jolt of energy.

"Come, let us walk together through the orchard as we did in our youth."

Obe looked over at Mason, silently requesting his permission.

Mason grinned and said, "Lovely! Enjoy your visit together. Cornelael and I will show Tony how the angels prepare the juice."

As Obe and Abigail walked off, hand-in-hand, Mason shuffled Tony in the direction of a giant juice press.

"If you thought it comical the way my brother angels played Sky Ball, wait until you see their antics in juice preparation," Cornelael said cheerfully.

Tony cracked a smile, and gazed back at the re-united duo before they disappeared into the pomegranate orchard. *Gee, hope this chance encounter helps to soften him up. I can see God attends to everything and everyone.*

Tony's eyes filled with hope for Obe. However, something about their encounter made him curious.

He stopped to pose a question to Mason. "What was that all about? The way she touched him, the kind of energy that came out of her. Certainly different than what I have experienced here thus far."

"Hmmm, I see what you mean." Mason scratched his beard as he considered the question. "You know, God is love, and love is constant, like a current of electricity that can never shut off. It never forgets; it is like an indelible tattoo on the soul. Those who we have loved and those who have loved us in return—say, a personal love, for the lack of other words, can experience it here with greater feeling now through the Spirit."

This brought up another question, one which had been with Tony most of his adult life. "Does that mean we can have sex here in heaven?"

Cornelael laughed and flapped his wings. "Oh," he said boyishly, "you're in for a surprise." He thundered with laughter, inducing Mason to chuckle too.

The scientist explained, "You see, human sexuality is based upon procreation, in other words, a co-creation with God. He gave creatures a capacity for carnal attraction and for euphoric abandonment in the physical act, to encourage procreation of souls upon which to impart His abundant love.

"Frankly, though, He found it odd that the human species have such a preoccupation with sex and, more dramatically, recreational sex." Mason thought for a moment, picking his words carefully.

"Tony, it's hard to describe. The answer to your question is both 'yes' and 'no'. You have now experienced the euphoric effect touch has on each of us when we have contact. Here in the celestial realm, souls that we have great affection for and those we have loved in our places of origin can share profound euphoric moments consistent with romantic earthly coupling, but with exceedingly more sensual impact. It is something you will have to experience for yourself to truly comprehend its unique joy and pleasure."

As Mason concluded his explanation, they heard claps of thunder coming from the pomegranate orchard from the direction where Obe and Abigail had entered. Cornelael giggled, clapped his hands, and flared his wings.

"There you have it, Brother Tony. It appears that brother Obe and Abigail are experiencing the coupling of joy." He giggled again.

"W-wow," Tony sputtered. He was overwhelmingly happy for the two of them.

This feeling was suddenly followed by one of loneliness. He bowed his head and thought, *I wish I had the opportunity to share that with my wife.*

He longed even more profoundly for her, feeling their connection, although out of reach for now. He recalled the moments he had held her and their children, and admonished himself for taking them for granted. Reading his thoughts, Mason comforted him.

"Everything is of God's plan, Brother Tony." He patted his friend on the shoulder.

Cornelael had missed, or had blocked out this exchange, having walked ahead out of respect for their conversation. Now he pointed excitedly.

"There's the juice factory. See the children playing?" he shouted, unable to contain his excitement. Without waiting for a response, he flew to join them.

Tony gaped at the sight and whispered, "This is incredible," as a glorious scene unfolded before them.

A multitude of children and angels occupied the fields and filled the sky above them. All of them were running or flying around, squealing with laughter. Tony watched, amused, as they playfully shot water-gun-like apparatuses, bathing each other in the sweet red liquid.

Mason shouted above the joyful voices of frolic. "It's pomegranate juice," he informed Tony.

"Where did all these kids come from?" Tony asked.

"Don't they have parents here? I don't see too many adults."

"These are the unborn children of the universe and those who had their earthly lives shortened. Through the great love and mercy of our Divine Redeemer, their souls are brought here straightaway at death. Angels serve as their surrogate parents, teaching and playing with them, along with some of the parents who were once separated from them and now reunited."

"They are so happy. I feel the love."

Tony marveled at God's parenting. Mason explained how God provided them with the education they missed and eventually reunited them to their families and respective cultures. The angels took their responsibility seriously, filling them with knowledge and continuity. Guided by the Holy Spirit, they helped the children finally experience family love.

"The angels and the religious who have never parented have the opportunity to feel the joy of raising a child. Souls who were denied the opportunity to raise or have children can experience the joy of co-creation with God," Mason told him with a fatherly smile.

"Hey, look at that angel! He's being soaked with juice by hundreds of them. He can't stop laughing!" Tony said, overtaken with laughter too.

"Look closer." Mason pointed a smile on his face. "Does that angel look familiar?"

"Oh no, that's Cornelael! He's turned bright red from the juice." Tony could hardly stand from laughing so hard.

"You know he loves to provoke them. He has the blessed heart of a child himself," Mason chuckled, proud of his winged friend.

"You know, I think Brother Obe would enjoy this too." Tony sobered up at the thought. "He missed much of his childhood. His life contained a series of tragic events, and I believe that's what keeps him from accepting God's will."

"The care and love you show him is going a long way to help him with that," Mason replied gently.

"Mason, I hope the time he spends with Abigail will help him too."

"I do too."

Then Mason poked Tony and grinned. "Come, Tony. Let's play with the children while we wait his return."

Nineteen

OBERMYER, YOU HAVE NO idea how much I missed you. I longed for many Earth years to sit with you once more under the apple tree, as we did in our youth. The memory of our first kiss gave me hope through a life of brutality." Abigail gazed softly into his eyes. "Do you recall the day we played hide and seek? I confess I planned that."

"You did?"

"I wanted to kiss you. I knew my eventual fate, and wanted my first kiss to be with someone I had affection for." Abigail stroked his cheek tenderly, setting him aglow, as she continued.

"Oh yes, the memory never left me. I thought of you while I was alone in the forest. Thinking of you warmed me at night as I closed my eyes to sleep. I often wondered if you were okay and prayed for you. I dreamt that someday we would be re-united."

Her face went somber. "Obe, after you left they took me into the main house as a housemaid. That would have been fine, but my master had other ideas. Like so many other of his slave women, he took physical pleasure with me." She hugged herself at the memory, her brown eyes sad. "He frightened me so. At those times my mind ran to thoughts of us together, and how innocent and happy we were then, playing in the orchard."

Obe held her with an all-consuming love, which caused a booming clap of electric energy.

Her eyes lit up with an idea. "Obe, let us transform." In an instant, she had changed into an adult state, a beautiful and alluring young woman.

Obe goggled, then stammered, "I...I don't know how, or if, I can do that."

"Just think of it, and it will happen."

Obe mused on how he would have looked had he grown to adulthood, and in an instant transfigured.

His face in wonderment, he felt his body with his hands. "Oh my, this is something. How do I look?"

Abigail took his hand and they sprinted, as they had done as children, and stopped before a still pool of water. She knelt at its edge first. "Come look. Look into the pool."

He knelt beside her and peered into its still depths. The reflection staring back at him was...

"My dear Lord... I... me... I'm... han... handsome..." he breathed.

"Yes, very much so." Abigail's reflection grinned back at him.

They held each other again, which caused more bursts of energy. Scores of pomegranates dislodged from the weighted branches above as they shook. One rolled between them, and Abigail picked it up, laughing.

"I guess we shook heaven." Then she noticed a spot on the pomegranate. "Oh my, it's marked. What a curious thing."

"What?"

"This is impossible." She pointed to the fruit in her hand. "Look, it's blemished."

Obe bowed his head and reached for the fruit. "It's me."

"You?"

"Yes, I am the cause of the imperfections."

"I don't understand." She looked at him in bemused silence.

"You, know that feeling everyone is having, the disruption. Well I believe that's me too."

"How can that be? We are in the state of perfect eternal glorification."

"Not I, not yet, but it's not for the lack of Him trying." He turned sad eyes on his beloved. "Abigail, I love God so much. He has been so generous to me. He even provided me with Brother Tony, to accompany me on my journey here. And now you—special, precious you."

"Well, what is it then, Obe?"

He sighed. "I have a disagreement with Him."

Abigail laughed, "You have a disagreement with God? How can that be possible? How can you be here, if that were true?"

"That I don't know. My presence here apparently amounts to a 'schism'. Something that has not happened since the fallen ones were cast out at the time of our creation."

"Obe, this schism, what is it?"

"I guess I just can't accept that there are a multitude of souls who will, in the end, not be accepted here. Worse than that, doomed to eternal damnation."

Tony gasped. "I can't believe that word can be uttered here. Obe, I believe that Our Divine Triune God does not damn souls to hell," she said in a shocked whisper, trying to come to terms with what Obe had just said. She lifted his chin and gazed lovingly into his eyes. "I believe that they do it themselves. They have no room for love in their existence. God is love. Love cannot abide with, you know."

"Well, He has the power to breathe love into them. Doesn't He?"

"Absolutely, Obe. But then what happens to our free will? Free will allowed us to exist as individual, autonomous souls. Without it, I think, the gift of eternal life would be hollow. The sacrifice of the Most High, Our Lord and Brother Jesus, would have been in vain. His suffering and that of ours would not have merit. What we have here, how could we appreciate it?"

"I know, I guess I'm just stuck. It's a mystery to me that God has permitted this. He chose not to doom me into the eternal fire long ago. In fact, He has been more than merciful to me. Even now, He has sent me to abide with Mason Pringle, a great scientist and theologian, and before that, He gave me the counsel of many others to help me through my time at Paraclete City.

"Now He has given me to the care of Tony Romero. Ironically, He had *Tony* assigned to *me* for guidance at Level One. Tony accepts God without question; he has inspired me, and has shown me that a soul who has experienced earthly life with all its sinful pleasures can still attain redemption by his love and trust of the Creator. In contrast to me, who knew little of such things."

"Rejoice, Obermyer Coddington, my beloved friend!"

"Rejoice?"

She squeezed his hand. "God's ways are not our ways. We must trust that He has a purpose for you. Oh, dear, if you had any idea of how special you are! Obermyer Coddington, you just don't see it, but you will, I'm sure. Keep in mind that doubt is the cornerstone of faith. Without it, there can be no journey of discovery.

"Faith comes from seeking, trusting, and loving God. Even those souls who did not benefit from a formal religious teaching, agnostics and atheists included, have redemption through God's mercy for their capacity to love and their compassion for humanity. There are many here with us."

She paused to collect her thoughts. "I believe that a task may be given to you. Open your heart and let it take hold."

This has never occurred to me, Obe thought, awe-struck. As he took in her words of counsel, he whispered a grateful "thank you."

Her last words, though, churned in his mind. *A task?*

Abigail looked away, listening for something. Then she turned back, a smile on her face. "I must take my leave now. I sense your friends seek your return. Our visit has given me great joy, and I look forward to us sharing eternity together. Peace and joy, my brother."

Abigail held him tightly for a parting moment, which initiated more loving sparks, then disappeared in his arms. Obe remained for a second, left with a longing for her.

Twenty

WITH A QUICK THOUGHT OF the others, Obe instantly materialized next to them, in the midst of frolicking kids and angels. The busy little souls were hysterical with laughter, but at once focused their attention on Obe, who they drenched with the sweet red juice in welcome.

After giving him electrified hugs, a few led him, now laughing heartily, to a water slide, where he careened down with them into a large pool of nectar and took on its color.

Amphibious creatures of all shapes and other fish-like entities similar in form to earthly dolphins played with Obe, dunking him and then catapulting him into the air with squeals of joy.

Nearby Cornelael, consumed with excitement, did mid-air somersaults. Obe shook with laughter as Cornelael swooped down to rescue him from the playful attacks.

"Brother Obe, isn't this the most wonderful joy? The children exude the great love that comes from God," Cornelael said, as he transported his now-tinted friend to the others.

Obe cried, "Great angel of God, I am filled to capacity with unbridled happiness!"

"Wow!" Tony said with a giggle at the comical sight of the multi-colored boy landing at his feet. "Obe, you're glowing," he chuckled.

"I have never experienced such joviality," Obe hiccupped, wiping the hair from his eyes.

"Give me a break, buddy. The word is 'fun'."

"Yes, fun." Obe smirked. "'A rose by any other name...'"

Mason joined the conversation. "This is a mere fraction of the delights that await you here at every turn. You have only been on the outskirts of the heavens thus far." He swept his arm to encompass everything they could see. "You could say this is an orientation plane of sorts. There are many other dimensions, or plateaus, in the Heavenly realms."

Tony shook his head in wonder. "It is inconceivable that Heaven contains things greater than this. I feel like I'm overflowing inside," he said with great appreciation. "When the little girl and boy touched my head while we were playing, I felt an even deeper love. I thought of my children, who are about the same ages."

Cornelael vibrated the ground with another roar of laughter. "Oh, wait my brothers! The closer you get to the Throne the more glorious you will feel. Praise to the Father, Son and Holy Spirit!"

"Really? I wish I could describe this."

Mason replied jovially, "Again, favored son, soon you will speak and hear in the language of the Holy Spirit, a language without words, in a 'state of knowing'. The tongue of God which, like Him, incorporates all means of expression, all the sciences, and infinite wisdom."

Tony and Obe bobbed their heads in awe.

"So, Obe, how did your visit go with Abigail?" Mason inquired with a grin.

This question brought Obe back to wherever his over-awed brain had taken him. "Wonderful! We had a most wonderful visit, thrilling and loving."

"Yeah, we heard the cannons thunder," Tony teased.

"Humans..." Cornelael quipped, shaking his head in mock disbelief.

Mason laughed quietly while Obe blushed with embarrassment.

Their lightheartedness halted as three huge streaks of light appeared in the sky, followed by the sounds of angelic choirs singing. The flashes of light transformed into the presences of three Archangels: Michael, Gabriel, and Pinchot. Gabriel sounded his trumpet, whose melodious tones caused a vibration that stirred within them.

Archangel Pinchot addressed the assembly.

"Blessed children of the Father of the Universe, you are beckoned to the Valley of Contemplation," he announced.

Archangel Michael also lifted his hands to address them. "Praise is to the Most Holy Infinite Triune God for you, His loyal children. Our Lord and Master, Divine Son of the Creator, will address you there with great love and affection. As you proceed, prepare with great anticipation in your souls to behold Him in His majestic wonderment."

"Isn't that your guardian, Pinchot?" Obe whispered to Tony.

"Yes, it is." Tony was almost speechless.

"Wow, he's just as beautiful and glorious as the others, isn't he?"

The three angelic creatures dissolved into the golden light, heralded again with the sound of Gabriel's horn and the chanting of angelic choirs filling the air.

"Yes. They are all so magnificent! Their beauty is mystifying."

Cornelael's face flushed at the compliment. A praise for one angel was a praise for all.

Mason seemed surprised at what had just happened.

"This is highly unusual. Never before have we been beckoned thusly. I believe God's plan is soon to be revealed concerning this disruption we've been feeling. Let us be off, for we have other stops on our way there."

"Why do you think He's called us now?" Obe asked with some trepidation.

"Are you beginning to fear a final confrontation?" Tony snickered.

Obe did not see the humor, and let Tony know. "Anthony Romero, have you no compassion? You think I do not know the gravity of my situation...risking the loss of this tranquil and peaceful life of abundance?" He raised his voice, "And not to mention the reality of the eternal furnace!"

"Cool your pits, Obe. My thoughts *were* about your feelings. I guess it just came out wrong. I'm sorry."

Mason interceded in an effort to defuse their tension. "Obe, we can stop at the dwellings of your parents on our way, and I've planned a surprise visit with someone very special."

Obe nodded, very interested.

"Mason, is there time for all that?" Tony asked Mason.

Cornelael giggled as Mason took on the task of explaining.

In his best Professor's Voice, he stated, "Time is relative here; actually, it doesn't exist. We only relate to it for the benefit of newcomers or those in the state of orientation and adjustment, and of course when we visit the earthly domains and other planets where life is transitory."

With an impish smile, Cornelael handed Tony a gold watch. Its face showed no numbers or dials, just an engraving of a chalice with the host above it.

Tony peered down at the timepiece with puzzlement. "Um...thanks?"

Cornelael laughed loudly. He ribbed Tony as he fastened the watch to his wrist. "Beloved Brother, wear this as a reminder, a remembrance," he chuckled.

Once again, a magical coach appeared before them. Obe got in first and drifted into a state of introspection, trying to absorb what he had learned.

Twenty-one

THE COACH CAME OVER THE CREST of a hill, which was blanketed with even more exotic species of bright green grasses. They highlighted beds of daisies, which sang in the gentle wind. The travelers had arrived at the precipice of a valley, and in the near distance, a shimmering, cross-shaped city came into view. It basked in illuminated shades of the rainbow, with dwellings constructed of crystal. Tony placed his hand on his heart at the sight of it.

"Mason, it's spellbinding, remarkable. People on Earth could never imagine such as this, not in a million years."

Mason had a soft smile on his face. "You know, loyal son of God, my eyes never tire at the sight of God's Divine architecture and the love that emanates from it."

Tony touched Obe's hand to awaken him from meditation. "Obe, look at what beauty has opened out before us."

Obe gasped in awe. "A wonder," he whispered.

In a very short time, they entered through crystal arches and found the city bustling with souls. Citizens whose robes dazzled with varying shades of pink, gray and yellow bustled along its streets. Angels flew above, singing and playing harps and lyres, which accented the scene.

The little angels, excited at the sight of Cornelael, rushed towards them and embraced him. They playfully lifted him up into the air while performing aerial acrobatics. Cornelael gathered them to his bosom, laughing.

Citizens happily saluted them as they passed down the main thoroughfare of Crystal City. Moments later, they found themselves before an immense Romanesque fountain. At its base, souls had gathered around two speakers clad in sparkling white robes.

As they made way to join them, Mason exclaimed with surprise, "It's the blessed Cecilia, and her husband Valerian!" He grinned and added with great affection, "These are blessed Roman martyrs from the third Earthly century A.D."

Mason went on to explain that Cecilia was a young Christian patrician who had married a pagan named Valerian. They had both been members of the upper class, and very wealthy. Cecilia had converted her husband to the Christian faith. After his baptism, they had practiced their Christianity openly. Their palace became a house-church for the Christian community.

Cecilia and Valerian had given their possessions away to the poor. They had refused to participate in public worship of the emperor or sacrifice in his honor. Therefore, they had been considered disloyal to the state.

Valerian had been arrested and executed. Cecilia had defied Roman law in order to bury him, and had continued to practice her Christian faith publicly. She became such a threat that the Roman Prefect had kept her under house arrest. With adamant one-minded belief, she had refused to sacrifice to the gods, and had received the ultimate sentence: to expire by suffocation, in her own bathroom. Cecilia had survived her three-day confinement in the steam room, but later had been beheaded, martyred in her own house.

"She and her husband now make their home in the Crystal City, also known as the City of Martyrs, a place occupied by many others who had suffered a similar earthly fate," he concluded.

"What courage they had! Special souls indeed," Tony said. He glanced at Obe; the boy was standing quietly, his lips pinched together. Tony hoped that that expression was one of agreement.

"Yes, special...and no different than the two souls who stand before me."

Tony and Obe both spun to see to whom Mason was referring. Mason placed his hands upon their respective shoulders. "It is the both of you. You have given your Earthly lives in sacrifice for God's children. Martyrs too, in every sense."

"Us? Me?" Obe said, doubt heavy in his voice.

Tony raised his brows at what Mason had said.

"What I did was automatic. What anyone would do. Nothing heroic about it," Tony objected.

"Yeah, same with me. Anyone would have done the same," Obe agreed.

Mason did not reply, but just smiled fondly.

Cornelael landed in a haphazard motion before them, wrestled down by the smaller angels. The little pranksters then embraced Mason, Obe, and Tony before they swiftly ascended to assault other visitors with their affection.

"Come my brothers, and see the places that Our Lord Jesus has prepared for you for completion of your missions." Mason placed his hands upon their shoulders once more, and they instantly appeared in front of a crystal mansion adorned with bricks of gold and doors of pearl; a design akin to Frank Lloyd Wright's famous Fallingwater home.

The mansion had cantilevered panes of crystal that extended from a hillside and seemed to float in mid-air. The dwelling nestled within a canopy of exquisite greenery, which was abundant with unusual three-dimensional flowers such as the human eye has never seen. A transparent structure, it blended with the surrounding forest as it sat atop a slow-flowing waterfall. The silver water ran into a pool before trickling down a laughing brook, enhancing the lush wilderness around it.

"Tony, Cornelael will tour with you through this glorious dwelling while I escort Obe to his," said Mason. Then both he and Obe disappeared.

Tony and Cornelael proceeded to the entrance.

"Wow! It is inconceivable that I am worthy of this!"

"This awaits all of God's faithful children. Come, there are those who expect you," Cornelael said tenderly.

The doors automatically opened to expose an elaborate atrium, back-dropped by a view of a vibrant forest, where Tony's grandparents awaited. He cried out in happiness and ran to them. When he tried to take them in his arms, they raised theirs instead, and flashed out beams of energy that almost knocked him over with feelings of profound love.

"Praise is to God for you, our little Anthony," they welcomed in unison.

Suddenly, visions of future events unfolded before him like holographic transmissions.

"Look, Tony. See how we will enjoy our family and company of friends for eternity."

Revealed for Tony were futuristic snapshots of joyful family gatherings and intimate moments with his wife and children. As his relatives gave him a tour of the mansion, the image display followed them into every room, showing snapshots of future events that would take place within them.

"Grandma, this is mind-boggling," Tony breathed. "No one can ever imagine this splendor or feel creditable of it."

"You know Anthony, how thrilled we were with color TV? Remember, we all went to Macy's when I bought it," his grandfather recalled. "We drove that salesperson crazy, repeatedly asking questions about its features. Here we not only see in Technicolor, but we live in it, and in dimensions of it in the embodiment of the Spirit." He chuckled. "No technology needed here, so no wrestling for the remote either."

Tony and his grandparents laughed at the fond memory.

"Grandpa, this is really amazing!" Tony said after the tour. "You know, this home is exactly what I would have designed, if I had had the power to do so."

"Well my son, I think you did, with the Divine Spirit as your builder."

Cornelael interrupted, "Praise is to God for you, loving Sister and Brother Romero. However, we must be off for now, to join the others."

Tony tried to hug them again, but as before, he simply received more bursts of joyful energy. Then he was gone, whisked away with Cornelael.

Twenty-two

ANGEL CORNELAEL, WITH TONY IN TOW, landed in front of another Crystal Mansion. This one sat in a picturesque colonial setting. Its architecture modeled that of an antebellum-period Southern plantation, and adorned with shrubs, trees and flowers of every conceivable type. The palatial home overlooked a grove of fruit, olive, and Persian date palm trees.

Also standing tall were live oak trees dressed in bright garlands of Spanish moss that climbed to their tops. These giants were enhanced by other flowers and plants that Obe would have recognized from his time, like wisteria, roses, and rambling, flower-laden vines. They clung to the trunks of the trees, which stood like columns along both sides of a path that led to a turquoise lake. The air was fragrant with vibrant azaleas and unusual jasmine-like scents.

"This is it, Cornelael? This is Obe's place?" Tony turned slowly, gazing with awe at the beauty around him. "I am not going to even attempt words."

"Praise the wonder of God, Tony," Cornelael replied in agreement.

They made their way through the entry hall, the centerpiece of which was a beautiful crystal chandelier. It was festooned with likenesses of cherubs holding flaming candles, each one emitting a soft, golden light.

They found Mason and Obe in the midst of a discussion in the parlor. Tony overheard Obe still defending his opposition to God's will.

"Still at it, Obe?" Tony questioned as they walked in. "Hah, I am beginning to believe that nothing will convince you. You have such a deep resentment that you just can't let go of it." Tony delivered his sarcasm with a wrinkled brow.

Obe reacted with fury, as if a different personality had surfaced, and retorted, "How can you judge me? You, with the plank in your eye! Especially you, who has lived a life..."

Before he could express his angry feelings, a sound of a driving wind interrupted him. In the blink of an eye, six towering spirals of light surrounded them. At once, they found themselves catapulted through a tunnel of light, after which they landed in an inhospitable, desolate, and cold place.

They came to their feet on a colorless dusty surface, under a sky filled with billions of blinking stars.

Tony shivered, both from the sudden cold and from the shock. "Oh my God, Obe, where are we?"

Obe was about to answer, but stopped once again at the sight of the six lights of energy, which transformed into figures of defender Angels, dressed in battle regalia and brandishing swords. The Angels took positions around them, glowing lanterns in their hands. Obe and Tony could now clearly see the extent of the true barrenness of this place to which they had been transported.

An Angel came forth to speak. Through the glow and aura, they saw golden shoulder-length hair and piercing jet-blue eyes, and recognized him as Archangel Gabriel.

"Praise is to Our Divine Lord for you, brothers Obermyer and Anthony. Be not afraid. I am the Messenger of God, Defender of the Throne, and Soldier against the Sons of Darkness. You were escorted here to continue your judgmental discourse."

He paused and bowed, cracking a moderate grin. "An appropriate space for you to exhibit your childlike human emotion without disturbance to the peace and sanctity of the heavenly realm. You will be under our protection while you are here, for as much time as it takes for you to resolve your conflict."

"You see, you've gotten us in trouble," Tony snapped. Obe just stared at nothing in particular, uneasy.

"Praise is to God for you, Archangel Gabriel, and your kind contingent of heavenly cohorts," Tony answered, in all humility. "Where, may I ask, are we?"

"You are on the dark side of the Earth's moon. No finer setting for the tone of your discussion."

Gabriel pulled back, leaving Obe and Tony in dimmer light. Tony fumed with even more frustration at Obe's obstinance.

"You see?" he lashed out at the boy. "More proof of God's love and mercy for you! He called you to His bosom, constantly, with persistence. But apparently you have no ears to hear or eyes to see, as I believe it was once said."

"Who are you, Anthony Romero, to judge me?" Obe snapped. "One who has led a materialistic and decadent life, with a deaf ear to God? What suffering have you endured? What losses have befallen you? Does one act of sacrifice make you a speaker for God and entitle you to the gift of Heaven? While other souls are doomed to eternal damnation, many of whom had also sacrificed themselves thusly?"

"Wow, listen to that. Wow, get it out, why don't you?" Tony flung back with a wave of his hand. "I guess two hundred Earthly years in Purgatory has done little to defuse it. Maybe that is the key to it all, Obermyer Coddington, and maybe those fallen souls you defend have a problem with anger too--anger that comes from a jealousy of not having God's power. Could it be you suffer from it too? The real issue here, however, is simply how you can question God's authority!"

Obe roared back at him with fury. "I love God, and probably understand Him more than many others! I have always marveled at the beauty of His creations and His goodness revealed to me through others in my life. It sustained me on earth, with visions of nature, its balance, and nourishment for land and people alike."

"Here we go again. Nobly said, but how can you relate to God in such a beautiful way on one side, and at the same time take this oppositional-defiant position of non-acceptance?" Tony glared at Obe, then deflated, his anger dissipating. He sighed deeply with a tremble to his voice.

"You know, you're right," Tony continued in a low voice. "I did lead a materialistic life, and had a nominal relationship with God. It baffles me that He has found me worthy of this. Me, of all people, abiding with saints and angels and with loyal souls like you who have had a real relationships with Him and who have a much greater capacity to understand His love and mercy."

Tony sought the angels with his eyes to gain insight from them. Obe bowed his head, touched by his humble words.

Tony spoke once more, with an ache in his voice, "You know how it troubles me, trying to comprehend this assignment we have with each other. Yes, each other. We are the ones that don't fit. You carry the dark spot on your tunic, and I carry another curiosity of unrest inside that questions my worthiness and purpose in all this."

Obe's eyes filled with tears at Tony's humility and listened.

"I think about my life on earth, and whatever befell me there pales in comparison to what you and millions of others have endured. True heroes of life in every sense. I agree with you, it is hard to believe that one act absolved me of my sins, the greatest being indifference to God-- not to mention to the example of Our Lord's teaching, suffering, and crucifixion for us on earth.

"Obe, like you, I have not been fully inducted. I carry a dark spot in my character too. It's just not visible. Have you noticed that I have not been able to hug people here? They flash kisses of energy and disappear."

Still wiping tears, Obe cracked a smile at Tony's dramatic way of speaking.

"Somehow, though, I think we are a key part of some greater plan that God has in motion. I know neither of us has been saintly. However, God has done much with others of our status, the Apostles for example. We need to put our doubts aside as they did, and wholeheartedly trust. Especially us, who have seen God's Divine Kingdom, with our own eyes."

Obe wept, overcome with great emotion, as he apologized to Tony. "Please forgive me for my harsh words," he said, choked with emotion. The boy buried his head in Tony's chest.

The moment was broken by the sound of scuffling. The angels had extended their swords, slashing them into what appeared to Tony and Obe as ominous shadows of dark spirits that had surrounded the Angels. Gabriel protected Tony and Obe by wrapping them within his wings, and with unimaginable speed, he transported them out through a tunnel of light.

Twenty-three

WITH A CRACK OF THUNDER, they landed moments later. To their relief, a profound peace instantaneously supplanted their previous fear.

Gabriel opened his wings to a splendid view of a thick forest of trees and an unusual variety of plants. Their silky leaves shone with deep vibrant hues contrasted by brilliant tints. The air was filled with the sound of flowing, tranquil water coming from the midst of the trees.

Gabriel bowed with reverence. "Obermyer Coddington," he directed, "take this path before you to seek further revelation."

The angel then bowed a farewell to Tony. "Praise is to God also for you, Anthony Romero, a messenger of God in your journey here and there."

"Thank you. Praise and glory is also to God for the Great Messenger and Defender of the Throne," Obe replied. They returned Gabriel's bow.

Gabriel vanished in a whirlwind and a clap of thunder.

"My God, Obe, the love in him! It just pierces your soul. They are awe-inspiring, these angels--all unique and different, but each with profound loyal natures." Tony sighed, with both happiness and relief.

One thing bothered him though. He asked Obe, "But what did he mean by 'Messenger of God', and 'in my journey here and there'? Sometimes I think it means that they will send me back. But I've already been buried, so..." He shrugged.

"I don't know, Tony. Remember, the concept of time here is ambiguous; existence, we have found, is on a continuum."

Obe rubbed his belly. "Tony this may sound funny, but all of a sudden I am hungry...very hungry."

"You must be kidding. There's no need for food here."

"I know. Peculiar, isn't it? Come, let us take the path."

"Yes. I would like to see the river we hear singing in the distance. I guess we'll find Mason and Cornelael somewhere on the way. You know Obe, now that you mention it, I'm starting to have grumblings in my stomach too. It must be the power of suggestion."

"Mine has increased. As if I had not eaten in days."

As they walked down the path, they had a chance to talk about their recent experience.

"Quite a trip we just took, wasn't it? A scary place, cold and dark without life. What a contrast to here. And the angels--who or what were they fighting?"

"Demons, I suppose."

"I'll tell you Obe, the salvation process is no joke. People on earth, me included, have had a penchant for denial; we avoid all the signs, especially the ones that require accountability. We cast them off as coincidences and superstition. This is serious business. Oh my Lord, if I had it to do all over again."

Obe nodded and exhaled loudly in a "whoosh". "No kidding."

As they proceeded down the path, the sound of the water got louder. Soon they heard voices and headed in the direction of the sound. As they got closer, they caught a glimpse of the voices' owners.

They stopped and peeked through the trees, and were amazed to see Cornelael, Mason, and a beautiful woman seated atop boulders of light at the edge of the river. The young woman had a breathtaking, statuesque presence, with an unusual bronze complexion. She was dressed in a yellow tunic that seemed to shine with its own light. They were surprised to see her roasting a fish.

"Don't be shy," she called out to them without looking up. "Come and quell your hunger. Join us here in peace. We mean you no harm."

"Sounds kind of familiar, doesn't it Obe?" Tony said in a low voice.

Obe replied with urgency, "Yes it does. Let us join them." His stomach gurgled an agreement.

The trees and floral vines parted in welcome as they made their way through to the water's edge. As they joined the trio, they could see the City of Celestial Vision behind them. It formed a backdrop, silhouetting Cornelael and Mason.

"You found us," Mason hailed with a fatherly smile. He gestured toward the woman. "This is..."

Obe interrupted him.

"I know who she is," he said with a smile. .He approached her and said, "Praise is to our Divine Lord for you, Pauline, sweet daughter of Elijah Thompson."

"And praise is to God for you, martyred son of the Most High and our earthly protector, Obermyer Coddington," she replied, a warm smile making her face glow. "Sit here in peace. Take this fish and eat without dread. Feel how you nourished a lost and hungry family, and know now how your words of kindness lifted our spirits with hope on our uncertain journey to freedom."

Obe accepted the roasted fish, which she had plated on a broad leaf. Each bite he consumed stirred a reflective vision in him of their backwoods journey together.

"The sweetest of all fish," Obe declared. It was clearer than ever to him, and his mind brimmed with the awareness of how he had helped revive her family--how he had called to them from the depths of the colonial forest and had fed them. The morsels of fish satiated him with, most of all, the fullness of love and tears of happiness.

"Praise is to Our Lord Jesus, for our rescue and salvation, through the vessel of your loving spirit and through your reception of His will. Although now, He suffers for us once more even here in His Kingdom." She paused with reverence, her eyes consulting the sky, and then pointed to Obe's tunic.

"The stain that has marked you, and all of us now, is His blood, which flows once more for salvation, that of yours and those for whom you seek it. Those souls who do not pursue redemption for themselves and disallow their capacity to love.

"The misguided who you vie for only thirst for ultimate power at the expense of both their own salvation and of those they encourage thusly. They give no thought to the needy and disenfranchised," she said with sadness.

Then her eyes turned to Tony.

"Anthony Romero, Praise is to God for you. Come, eat, and be blessed with the satiation that can only come from God, the Eternal Fisherman."

Tony accepted the fish with gratitude. He broke off a piece and placed it in his mouth, and as he did so, he heard a voice: "Will you do the work of My Will?"

Tony's eyes widened as if he had seen a ghost. The others looked up at the woman, seeking clarification.

"Anthony, what you have eaten is now part of you. It will nourish you on your journey as it did ours. Be at peace."

Pauline generated a beam of light into him, raised her hands, and bestowed a blessing. Tony felt a jolt of profound peace, which filled him with strength and courage.

Coming to her feet, she embraced Obe, which elicited a rumble of thunder similar to that which he had experienced in the pomegranate orchard. He stood immobilized, receiving the depth of the love he felt in her arms.

She then took her leave, disappearing into the forest with an affectionate wave of her hand. Cornelael spread his wings with childlike joy, and Mason bowed with great respect as they saw the wake of her glowing light dissolve into the trees.

While their eyes still beheld the remnants of her glow, they suddenly heard the sound of a trumpet. They turned their attention toward the river, and saw a Romanesque barque, gilded in gold leaf, awaiting them. Angels lined its floral rails and bid them to board, calling out with poetry and song.

When they crossed over the barque's jeweled gangway, Tony noticed something odd about his reflection in the river, and stopped to look more closely. What he saw shocked him.

"My dear Jesus! My tunic is also now stained with the mark!"

Mason consoled him, "My dear brother, be not alarmed. For you, it marks courage and solidarity with the Will of the Divine One. In time, we will know its meaning, and I am positive that it will be of great significance. Come now, let us be off. We are awaited at the City of Celestial Vision, the abode of prophets."

Mason pointed. "Look, it sits there on the horizon."

Twenty-four

A CENTER-MASTED SAIL, one of red silk embroidered with a golden cross, propelled the elaborate vessel. With effortless ease, it transported them towards the heavenly City of Celestial Vision. At one point, the river narrowed into a spectacular canal, where a Venetian-like urban center stretched out before them.

People in multi-colored tunics strolled the thoroughfare, and others on balconies in view of the sparkling canal waved in welcome. Angels frolicked above them, playfully doing aerial acrobatics with a flock of white doves.

"Wow, Obe! It's hard to believe that we will soon reside here." Tony couldn't decide what to gaze at first.

"He promised us, but for me, coming from a remote two-room farmhouse, it's still hard to imagine," Obe said. He ran his hand along the seat. "I mean, just these cushions we are sitting on! Goodness sake, our beds were made of straw!"

Tony's brow furrowed at his friend's words. He sighed and shook his head.

"I believe that the words of your rescued friend, Pauline, did not convince you," Tony prodded. "Am I right? You're still not convinced?"

Obe thought to himself, *If I only knew why.*

Tony was about to prod him again, but Mason interrupted with a change of subject.

"Wait till you see what's up ahead," he said with excitement.

The Angel helmsman engaged the rudder. The sail adjusted, and a swift breeze pushed the boat into a channel that forked to the right of the canal. This brought them in eye view of the skyline of the City of Celestial Vision. They sucked in their breath at its beauty, enhanced by the luster of Throne City in its distant backdrop.

A cluster of Angels flew above. Some swooped down upon them, with a flock of doves at their heels, to bid them farewell.

Cornelael sighed with joy as his eyes fixed on the horizon.

"Here are the great Prophets, inspired shepherds of courage who willingly sacrificed for God," Mason said with wonder.

"Will we see them?"

"Oh yes, brother Obe. They host what you'd call a 'town square meeting' at the Forum of Messengers.

"Many who attend are bound for places in the Universe, into uncharted domains ripe for evangelization. Domains where creatures of intelligence reside; those souls who have not heard the good news, although spiritually capable."

A frown creased Tony's forehead. Puzzled, he asked, "Mason, are you saying that people still work here?"

"If they wish, very much so."

Obe joined in. "What do you mean, 'spiritually capable'?"

Mason answered him, "Everything is God's creation. All is of His seed and all elements of life come from Him, like that of humans who inherit the genes of their parents. In God's case, it is His spirit, which lies within all living things. That spiritual part of them yearns for Him on an unconscious level.

"For example, have you not felt at times, say, when events were going well in your earthly lives, when you felt great satisfaction that a longing still existed for something greater and deeper? You might call it a 'want for completeness'. It's the soul wishing to return to the consciousness of God and His Divine well of love and tranquility."

"Well then, with that seed implanted, why would not God accept the return of all souls?" Obe snapped with frustration.

Mason maintained his patience and gently went on with his explanation. "You see, my brother that is where the exercise of free will engages. Our souls are egotistical in nature. They are bent on the need to survive. However, they mistake that drive for the longing to return God as something of their own contrivance.

"They yearn to aggrandize themselves with wealth and power, but not for God. What results is that they go against their inborn spiritual nature. In essence, they discount the Word of God, His merciful signs and gifts, and reject His Love, thus becoming entrenched in a sinful state."

"I get it," Tony said. "This may be simplification, but I think it's like when you know deep inside that what you're about to do does not feel right but you do it anyway, and because it is forbidden it adds greater excitement to the act."

"Yes," Mason agreed. "That moment of uncontrolled carnal excitement is where you find the work of evil and the negative encouragement of the same. Those souls that continue in this manner, in the end, lose all sense of the Spirit. They are darkened by the absence of welcome for God, becoming more and more distant from Him."

Tony and Obe nodded in agreement, and continued to listen to Mason with a keen focus.

"They refuse to search for Him in their doubt. Instead, they adopt a willful thought process that ultimately blocks the light of His love and mercy. This intrinsic line of thought encourages them to detour, in effect serving to carry them away by a flattering conglomeration of exciting transgressions.

"These willful actions can accumulate and meld into a lifestyle of irreparable sin and darkness. The struggle of faith in the human form is extraordinary; it calls for a purge of our formidable human nature.

"The Divine Apostle and Saint, Paul of Tarsus, defined this struggle when he spoke to the Roman people: '*I do not do the good I want, but the evil I do not want, is what I do. For I delight in the law of God in my inmost self, but I see in my members another law at war with the law of my mind and making me captive to the law of sin which dwells in my members.*'"

Cornelael had been listening intently to Mason's explanation. With a pious bow, he offered a perspective as to why saintly souls in heaven choose to continue their mission. "Princes of God, the prophets you will hear speak, although in perfect peace in this realm of the Triune God, do at times give up this tranquility to further glorify God.

"They work to harvest the souls that abide in the multidimensional universes that abound in God's creation, and also train others who have a similar vocation, to minister to those entities who know not God, to seek their ultimate salvation."

"Kind Mason Pringle, is this not God's heaven?"

"Yes, Obermyer, it is in a material form, with real solidarity, and affirmed by the resurrection of our Divine Lord and the assumption of our blessed Mother, witnessed by us here. However, the heavenly kingdom is also nonmaterial and spiritual, existing everywhere; every particle of creation and planetary system is embedded with God's Spirit."

As they reflected upon Mason and Cornelael's words, they heard the voice of the boat's Angelic Captain: "Hark, beloved children of God! Our arrival is at hand! Go with great joy; our tidings and those of the Angelic Choirs go with you."

Twenty-five

THE CRAFT GLIDED TO A STOP alongside a festively-lit pier lined with floral boxes. Blissful citizens, sitting around tables and walking along the pier, waved in welcome as they disembarked. At the end of the dock, they boarded a wheel-less ultra-modern tram.

In moments, they were transported into a large modernistic city, alive with crowds of people and angels in bright-colored tunics. The roads and skies were filled with inhabitants, both walking and flying, and on the streets were vehicles of every sort, just like a major city on earth.

They passed a large intersection marked by carved alabaster signs showing different places of gatherings, which prompted Tony to ask, "Mason, would I be correct to assume that the Forum of Messengers, like those other locations listed on the road signs I see, are all places of learning?

"Oh yes indeed, very much so. You see, besides the natural curiosity souls have about God's science, their profound love for Him moves them to share it. Thus they continue to learn how to act as vessels in harvesting souls, as the saints and prophets have done, both on Earth and in other planetary cultures in the millennia past."

"You know, I have those feelings already. I wish I could turn the clock back and touch the hearts of those I left behind," Tony said wistfully.

Mason did not answer, but Obe seized the opportunity to zing him.

"Well, Brother Tony, maybe now you have greater insight for the trouble I have in my heart. I too would like the redemption of all God's intelligent creatures."

Tony's lips quivered at this provocation and, trying to contain himself, countered, "Obe my dear friend, it's not the same thing. You just refuse to see the true picture. God did not reject them. It is they who rejected Him."

Cornelael distracted them by saying loudly, and with a bounce to his step, "I very much love the vigorous discussions at the Forum. I always gain more understanding of the natures of humans and other species." With hearty laughter he added, "The waffle sandwiches of ice cream that one finds here are alone enough to inspire souls to a deeper love of God."

Mason also laughed. "Beloved Archangel Cornelael, if you were of the human nature, you would have been a lifelong member of... what is it Tony? Weight...?"

Tony, smiling, completed his words, "Watchers. Weight Watchers."

Cornelael flapped his wings and they all enjoyed a laugh together.

The tram continued for a distance through a lush forest of evergreens. Everywhere they looked were bubbling streams and cascading waterfalls. The road opened up to a panoramic beach of sparkling pink sand, with a pyramid-shaped volcano in the vista.

The vehicle rose into the air and landed atop the mountain, where the Forum of Prophets Square sat in an amazing arboretum of spectacular plant life nestled in its crater, dotted with dwellings of majestic granite.

Tony was the first to speak. "Unimaginable beauty," he breathed.

Mason nudged Cornelael. "You know, kind friend, I have now also developed a yen for a waffle."

"What's a waffle?"

"I guess you would call it a form of pancake, Obe. A crisp version, with a pattern of indentations on both sides. Quite desirous," Cornelael answered with child-like enthusiasm.

As they disembarked the tram, Cornelael hurried them down a path that opened to a large floral garden with marble tables and benches. A yellow-and-red-canopied booth sat at its center, where Angels and celestial residents prepared a variety of waffles. The new arrivals noticed with tempted interest that some had fruits and others were covered with the creamiest ice cream. A holographic sign hung nearby, which listed an assortment of flavors named after saints and prophets.

Cornelael was the first to approach the booth. His fellow angels greeted him with a bow of admiration.

"Praise is to the Most High for you, Archangel Cornelael, loyal defender of the Throne," they said.

One of them pointed to the menu board. "What is your choice?" he asked.

"This is very difficult, but I think I would like to start with an Abraham."

The others were also welcomed, and they studied the exotic menu of waffles to make their selection.

Tony and Obe gave each other a high sign, eagerly anticipating their turn. However, the vast list of waffle combinations was making it difficult to choose. Mason noticed their difficulty and made a suggestion.

"It is a wonder for you, isn't it? Tony, I would start with a Joseph, which is somewhat like the Italian St. Joseph pastry namesake on earth. For you, Obe, you may wish to start with a Patrick, which has the magnificent flavor of whiskey cream."

Their eyes widened, and they nodded in agreement. Smiling, the Angels gracefully served them their choices. As they bit into their respective waffles, the flavor and aroma not only titillated their senses, but they also found that consuming them conjured up happy memories.

They sat together at a table surrounded by gardenias that gave off an exceptional aroma. As Tony and Obe ate, they noticed with surprise that the waffles regenerated themselves as they were being eaten. When they began to get a full feeling, the regeneration stopped.

Tony, consumed with laughter, remarked, "Harry Houdini, the famous magician, would marvel at this non-stop magic."

Jovial Cornelael nodded. "Oh, he has, and how! Quite a personality, I must say."

The sound of a gong resonated in the near distance and cut his words short. He looked toward the sound. "The forum is about to begin. Come, let us take our leave."

He pointed to a path made of perfect flagstone, placed atop a shimmering underlayment. The path opened up to a large town square with a simple granite podium at its middle, surrounded by an outdoor market and a theater with a marquis that listed coming events.

Angels ushered people in, and within moments, all were seated and the crowd became quiet. A choir of Angels descended in the midst of cascading rose petals and sang for the audience, their voices ringing throughout the square. Their melodious voices brought beatific smiles to the faces of the waiting participants.

After the choir finished and ascended, a floating platform, which rested upon a bed of glistening clouds, landed in the center square. The crowd reacted with jubilant applause.

Twenty-six

TRUMPETS SOUNDED AS Archangel Gabriel descended with outspread wings to the marble podium. "Eternal peace and joy is for you, beloved children of the Most High Triune God, Who is glorified by your love."

At that instant, a row of marble pedestals appeared, occupied by saintly ancient prophets. Around their heads were sparkling halos, and they were dressed in superb robes. The participants arose and bowed with great respect.

Gabriel stretched his arms out and announced, "This convocation is headed by great prophets; inspired leaders who, through their faith, advocated for the cause of the Most High in their cultural realm. Ultimate proclaimers, they led and taught, and by their actions brought others to grasp and understand the abundance of God's love. These are loyal advocates who sacrificed in ministry, often through a life of hardship and torment.

Gabriel looked over to them with eyes of reverence, then went on.

"The topic of our discussion at this conference is the presence and purpose of evil forces that still have an effect on certain cultural realms. Specifically, dark principalities, which through the mystery of God's will retain the power to enlist the destructions of souls."

He paused, and the sad look upon his face at the mention of evil was the same as the reaction of those in the audience.

"Before I introduce our learned speaker, I would like to alleviate the concern that has been growing in our divine home. I believe that you all know what I mean; the unease marked by 'red spots of blood', which have appeared upon your tunics. A blight of some sort, accompanied by a feeling of imbalance, and experienced here and now with greater intensity."

Obe buried his head in his hands, as if convicted by the Archangel's words. Tony, seated next to him, patted his shoulder as Gabriel continued.

"There is a soul amongst us who has initiated this break in Heaven's serenity, with God's knowledge. However, we must trust that God has a purpose for that soul, and ultimately for all of our fellow beings. One of God's many attributes is His mystery."

Gabriel laughed. "We never know what He is up to."

The assembled joined him in laughter. All but one.

Obe's eyes showed fear. "This is about me," he whispered.

Tony offered no response, knowing that whatever he said would fall on deaf ears.

Internally, Obe fired questions at God, his queries filled with irritation.

Why this elaborate assembly, Lord? Is this a method designed to convince me? How could I possibly be this important? Why not just dispose of me into the darkness and fire? Obviously I'm a burr in your saddle blanket, as it were.

He lifted his eyes, and with sadness and tears conjured the strength to re-focus on the Archangel's introduction.

"It is now my pleasure to present our renowned speaker, beloved Saint Augustine of Hippo."

Augustine appeared out of a cloud of multicolored mist. The audience rose with exuberant applause.

"Praise is to the Triune God for you, learned and humble teacher of the faith."

"And Praise is to God for you, humble Messenger and Defender of the Throne, Archangel Gabriel."

Augustine extended his hands to those before him, which exposed a stark red bloodstain on his silver gray tunic, eliciting gasps from those gathered.

"Heroes of the faith," he began as he surveyed the audience, "I understand that many of those present here have interest in serving God once again, as vessels of redemption in other diversified communities of His vast universe. It sounds tempting to me too," he added, stopping to smile. "However, I think I will take a few more millennia to bask here in His presence. And maybe enjoy a waffle or two more."

He chuckled, and everyone joined in.

"You know, I do recommend the 'Francis', with the embellished flavor of mascarpone cheese and candied fruits and nuts," Augustine said, and laughed again.

When the laughter from the audience had died down, he said, "Instead of having a lecture, I thought I'd ask for one of you to act as an antagonist, in debate, and pose questions about the problem of evil."

The attendees became eerily quiet at the second utterance of the word 'evil'. He took a breath and scanned the assemblage with his eyes. "Do I have a volunteer?"

The audience searched about with curiosity to see who would accept the challenge.

Tony and Mason were shocked as Obe stood and shouted, "I will!"

The people groaned when they noticed the spot of blood upon his tunic, which showed far larger than those that marked each of them.

"Please come forward, blessed son of God," Augustine answered him. Another podium emerged opposite him.

Obe proceeded down through the crowd while he spoke inwardly to God.

Okay, I get it. I accept the challenge. So let's bring this to a head, if this is what You want.

His face and attitude were defiant as he stiffly took his place at the podium. He gave a reverent nod to Augustine, Gabriel, and the Prophets.

Augustine began. "Evil is the most serious problem in the Universe, and the most serious objection to the existence of God. What is the first question you would like to visit, beloved son of the Creator?"

Obe pulled at his chin, and without further thought submitted his question, the one that had kept him from full communion with his Creator:

"Many souls have asked, 'If God is so good, why is His world so bad'?" Before that could be expounded upon, he added, "If an all-good, all-wise, all-loving, all-just, and all-powerful God runs the show, why does He seem to be doing such an awful job of it?"

"Oh, my God," Cornelael whispered. He cringed as Tony and Mason squirmed in their seats.

The audience reacted with expressions of shock and disbelief. After a moment, the Prophet Isaiah stood. He smoothed his snow-white beard, which complemented the glow that encased him.

"Great Augustine, learned teacher and servant of God, allow me a reply."

Augustine bowed in respect.

"First, I would like to remind all those present that what our brother Obermyer questions is what all of us, at some time in the process of conversion, have so lamented. Doubt is the foundation for a journey to faith, and ultimately to trust and acceptance of God. For those here who aspire to evangelize in other realms and dimensions of God's intelligent creation, please take note.

"One can assume that a person who made such an inquiry may have felt resentment toward God, and maybe not so much from the lack of evidence for His existence. Nevertheless, here in this plane the question of God's existence is inapplicable."

He counseled that when an emissary of God communicates with such an individual, it is important to remember that it is more like addressing someone with an estrangement rather than to a scientist seeking proof. He reminded them that the reason for unbelief could be described as that of an unfaithful lover, and not a matter of reason. The unbeliever's problem is not just a soft head, but also a hard heart. A good supporter knows how to let the heart, through example, lead the head.

Isaiah focused his loving eyes on Obe and answered:

"In actuality, our brother left out other questions, which are most often grouped with those he has visited: 'Is God the Creator of evil? Is He to blame for its existence?'

"As most of us have come to know, evil is not an entity or a being. All beings are either the Creator's or creatures created by Him, and everything God created is good.

"We naturally tend to picture evil as a material thing—a black cloud, etc. However, what we viewed misled us. If God is the Creator of all things and evil was a 'thing', other questions arise.

"The answer is 'no', because evil is not a thing but a bad choice, or the damage done by a wrong choice. One cannot perceive evil as anything other than negative, no different from the human disease of cancer. However, it exists, ever present, but not as a thing. However, its existence is also not an illusion."

The Great Prophet bowed and sat back down. Augustine glanced at Obe once again and was about to address him when Obe shouted out another question:

"Where did evil come from then?"

"Here he goes again, adding more nails to his own coffin. Please get him down," Tony pleaded.

Cornelael motioned to him with his hand to remain calm.

"Where did evil come from?" Augustine repeated and glanced for a response from the panel of prophets. One, a celebrated Sufi Mystic and Poet of the Islamic sect, stood and bowed.

"Allow me. I would like to answer this question."

Augustine nodded and introduced him. "Rumi Mevlana will provide an answer. He is known for his poetic contributions on planet Earth, circa 1273, which I share with you:

"I am God's Lion, not the lion of passion. I have no longing except for the One. When a wind of personal reaction came, I did not go along with it. There were many winds full of anger and lust and greed. They move the rubbish around, but the solid mountain of our true nature stays where it's always been."

Now at the podium, Rumi bowed with admiration. "Praise is to God for you, blessed Augustine, Teacher of the Church, and Archangel Gabriel, Defender of the Kingdom, and thank you for the kind remembrance.

"Let me begin. As we know, God is the source of all life and joy. Therefore, when the human soul rebels against God, it loses its life and joy. Now a human being is body as well as soul. We are all singularly distinct creatures--embodied souls.

"Given that, the body must share consequentially in the soul's inevitable punishment—-one ultimately natural and unavoidable. In comparison, it would be like bodily injuries that occur from jumping out of an airplane without the benefit of a parachute," he added with a chuckle.

"Therefore, we may conclude that the connection between spiritual evil and physical evil are as bonded together as the soul and the body. However, this brings up another question: If evil is founded in free will, and God is the donor of free will, isn't God then the originator of evil?"

The audience gasped. Unperturbed, he motioned them to calm, and went on.

"The Almighty gave us a portion of His power to exert our free will. Would we want Him to have made us as androids?"

Obe just itched to get into it, and raised his hand.

"May I..."

"Certainly, my brother."

"Haven't you ever felt that our Divine Lord, the King of Mercy, could spare the damned and offer them some form of rehabilitation? I have visited that dark and fiery place, and the thought of a soul suffering there for an eternity is inconceivable to me. Is it not true that mercy is the greatest gift when it is hard to give? Why then will He not relent?"

As Tony listened to the exchange, he became fearful for Obe. He butted his head with a fist.

Oh my God, he thought, *Obe, think of your soul. This is serious.*

"You see, my brother of profound love," Rumi answered him, "God's mercy has to be accepted, and as a prerequisite to that, each individual soul has to seek it by truly acknowledging Him, His will, as He acknowledges ours. I'm sure if we analyze each individual fallen soul's history we'd see God's hand of redemption and mercy in a lifelong pursuit of that soul's salvation.

"I agree, the worst of evil is eternal evil, there be it hell. In effect, what you suggest is that hell contradicts a loving, merciful, and invincible God." He swept his hand emphatically.

"No, in those cases to which you refer, their condemnation is a result from the exercise of free will. Souls freely choose hell for themselves; God does not cast anyone into hell against his or her will. If a soul chooses, out of free will, to say yes or no to God's love and spiritual communion, there is the possibility that the soul will say no, which is its choice and possibly in the end its ticket to hell."

The attendees confirmed with nods of the heads.

The Great Prophet went on to add, "Free will, in turn, was created out of God's love, a gift and a privilege bestowed by Him. Moreover, honored by Him, even to the extent of the pain He receives in the loss of a soul. It still remains a mystery to me if, in fact, God experiences pain of any sort, but I tend to believe He does."

He met Obe's eyes and spoke directly to him. "I continue to live in wonder, here in God's embrace. He is unpredictable, though His reason always proves impeccable and astounding. His mercy is eternal. Therefore, who knows what the future may bring for you and those lost souls you advocate for; prayer, as ever, is the bridge to healing."

He commended Obe for the depth of love and sensitivity he showed for his fellow man—and assured him that his prayers were with him. He told Obe that no one wanted evil to exist and that hell was just evil eternalized. He then concluded, "If there was evil, and if there was eternity, inevitably hell had to exist."

Obe, stunned by Rumi's discourse, bowed with respect and vacated the podium in deep thought. The audience also immersed itself in contemplative reflection.

Gabriel broke the moment. "Blessed citizens in Christ, the Forum has concluded. I know that this discussion has stirred your inner peace, and again I caution you: know that God's purpose will triumph here. His Will, for eternity, will prevail.

"On a lighter note," Gabriel paused with a smile, "You are all invited to remain here to enjoy a festival of dance, poetry, and music, along with a buffet of culinary delights, some of which come from Our Blessed Mother's garden. Praise is to God for you."

The crowd responded, "And also for you."

Mason and Cornelael rose to meet Obe as he came from the podium, while Tony, still troubled, sat shaking his head.

Mason announced, "I have a surprise for you both. We have received a very special invitation." His eyes twinkled. "Come, let us board the coach."

"Mason?" Tony asked, perplexed. "I thought we had been summoned to Throne City."

"Oh yes, my brother. The stop we now make on our journey is in preparation for that."

Cornelael added, "Kind of like your life's journey in seeking God."

Obe gripped Tony's hand and held him back from boarding the coach.

"You must think I'm dead awful by the questions I asked and the unrest I caused the people." Obe gazed sadly at his friend.

"No, Obe, I don't think you're awful. Far from it. As he said, you asked questions that have stirred in humanity since the birth of creation. Like me, I believe that many, if not all of us, struggled with harnessing our thirst for personal power. What occurred to me in your discourse with Rumi was that you seemed not to be advocating for the fallen, but for yourself instead.

"It may be that you are trying to retain a sense of power. Remember, most of your life had been tragic, with heavy losses--your parents, your friends, and your home--and then in the end your own life cut short. You suffered the impact of severe emotional events, all of which were out of your control; times of trauma that may have impeded your transition into adulthood."

Tony shared his recollection of what he learned in his College Psychology class.

"Our professor taught that adolescents who arrive at the brink of emancipation feel the loss of their childhood. They fear the future and having to take responsibility for themselves."

Obe stared at him as if he didn't know he had it in him.

Sounding more and more like a professor, Tony went on to explain that this stage required one to disconnect from dependency and to challenge the rules of one's parents, a traumatic time in itself.

"Obe, maybe at that crucial point your process of life change was interrupted by the tragedies that befell you."

Obe's head spun trying to digest what Tony said, but before he could question him Tony went on.

"You know, Obe, sometimes I believe we see God as if He were a model of a three-masted battlewagon. We focus on its sails, cannons and intricate details. We look at it in awe, with great respect for its construction and power. But we don't allow ourselves to consider how it lives in the elements, carrying and protecting its cargo, passengers and crew as it breathes the wind. I know you kept your faith, and can recognize how you can be angry with God."

Tony paused with a nervous back and forth sway, incredulous at what was coming out of his mind and heart. *Wow, where am I getting this from?* he asked himself.

He went on. "Obe, I heard it once said that it's hard to drain the swamp when you're up to your butt in alligators.

Think about it. Maybe it's the alligators you should be combating, not God?"

Tony admitted that it had been difficult for he himself to understand why God had given them such elaborate attention, and that he felt no different from Obe. Yet it occurred to him that they were in the process of preparation for something, so he further appealed to Obe.

"Don't you think? The mystery question is--why? Why are we given such importance? I mean really, we are two obscure souls, specks of sand in the greater scheme of things. Somehow though, I believe His purpose for us has greater implications than that of our unworthy salvation—a possibility? Yes?"

Tony swallowed, surprised at his own penchant for complex thinking, and spoke again. "I also suspect that our journey to salvation is still in process. We are *in* heaven but not *of* heaven. I suspect our purpose is yet to be fulfilled."

Obe snapped a response. "What are you suggesting? What use could He have for my perceived oppositional behavior?"

"Yes," Tony countered, "I guess that's what I have come to believe. I think He does, and I'm sure it will soon become known. Things have been moving fast for us since we met in the darkness of Paraclete City—I'm telling you there is a definite purpose here."

They suddenly realized that they had kept the others waiting, and hurriedly joined them with great anticipation for the next stop. Maybe there another piece of the Divine Mystery would be solved.

Twenty-seven

THE COACH ROCKED WITH the gentle sway of a baby's cradle pushed by a mother's hand. It progressed along its path accompanied by the sound of an angelic choir, which sung sweetly in their ears. Both Obe and Tony drifted into a meditation that emptied them of all concerns.

After a time, Obe's eyes cracked open, prompted by the feel of silk upon his face. He smiled at the sensation, and the scent of roses that accompanied it. His brows rose with anticipation, and he happily remembered, *My mother loved the scent of roses. I remember the times she would awaken me by tickling one under my nose.*

Tony, also now alert, widened his eyes and waved to test the silky air. Words escaped him again as he glanced at the others, whose faces held similar expressions.

Mason answered his unspoken words. "Yes, there is no suitable human vocabulary. Tony, in time, it will be easier for both of you to process these experiences as you adapt to the language of God's love."

Tony shook his head in wonder. "In reality, brother, spoken words are unnecessary here."

Before long, they passed under a trellised arch of exquisite roses, and a contingent of Archangels with regal presence received them on the other side. They wore white lustrous tunics, armored with golden breastplates and engraved with crosses. Cornelael stood, extended his wings as if in a military salute, and exchanged ceremonial bows to his fellow winged brothers.

In passing, Tony nudged Obe and pointed at the countryside. It had changed from lush illuminated greenery to a landscape of sand dunes, which sparkled with a pinkish hue and added to the magic. They wondered at its unusual beauty.

An enchanting oasis appeared before them; they marveled at the sight of clear pools of water, surrounded by clusters of olive trees and intermingled with exotic date palms. Interspersed among them were unusual cacti in blossom.

Still breathless, they came upon a stand of gigantic fir and cedar trees that together formed a cathedral-like appearance. The voices of frolicking children emanated from its confines, and they could hear the sound of the felling of trees.

Now in eye view, Tony said with amazement, "Listen! The falling trees, they sing as they float down." The trees landed upon the crystallized sand and rang out in symphonic notes of melody.

Obe asked with curiosity, "Why are they cutting down trees?"

Mason pulled his beard and answered, his own voice full of interest, "That's what it looks like. I do not know why, but I'm sure there is a divine purpose."

Tony chimed in, "Someone once asked me if heaven would be boring. That's a laugh."

Cornelael flapped his wings, and Tony quipped, "I didn't think it was that funny."

"Beloved son of God, sometimes humans ask the silliest things," Corneal replied. He laughed with more intensity at his own words, almost causing the coach to tip. Mason held on, chuckling at Cornelael's comic reaction, and offered his insight.

"It is odd to think that we humans could ever believe heaven was boring, especially with all the toil and suffering we endure on our earthly journeys. You'd think that we'd envision salvation at least as exciting, or more exciting in the positive way, than the level of pleasure experienced on earth. I guess it remains a question of trust."

Obe just shut his eyes at the mention of the word *trust.*

"I'll have to think that one through," Tony conceded, with an introspective scratch of his chin.

Soon they passed into a small ancient village and the coach, adding mystery to their experience, transformed into a cart. A pair of oxen pulled it now, and the animals smiled back at Tony and Obe as they gasped in amazement.

"What next?" Tony cried in bewilderment, finding himself seated now upon bundles of straw. He also noticed that they had all changed in physical appearance. Their tunics were gone, replaced by an older version of clothing, called *halugs*, woven from wool.

Feeling his face suddenly itchy, Obe rubbed at his face and was startled to feel a straggly beard. Likewise, Tony felt his own face, and found that he was similarly adorned.

Cornelael, who had become their driver, bellowed with laughter at their shocked reactions. He pulled at the reins and teased Tony, "Brother Tony, I guess you got the answer."

Mason explained that the houses and streets they passed were mirror images of ancient Israel at the time the Savior walked the earth. Cornelael stopped the cart in front of a tan-colored dwelling surrounded by a stone wall that created a central courtyard. Visible to them were a number of small rooms that opened off from it. The windows were covered by latticework and shutters that served to secure the building from the elements. Tony and Obe knew without being told that this was just for decoration, foul weather being non-existent in the sphere of Heaven.

Mason, tickled by their reactions, continued to elucidate as they got out of the cart. The courtyard gate opened, inviting them to enter.

"Look there, by the well. It's an ancient *mikveh*; yes, a ritual bath used for cleansing and purification before the Sabbath."

Mason pointed to a cooking area that contained a smoking wood-burning oven, supporting loaves of baking bread. Trying to remain reverently silent, he pantomimed the stir of a spoon, and motioned to a stone table where cooking utensils and implements for grinding grain lay. He raised his hands to the sky above to illustrate that most of the cooking took place outside.

Obe inhaled the aroma of the fresh-baked bread. "This reminds me of awakening to the smell of my mother's baking. You know, she also added rice to the dough to make the bread heartier and keep longer," he said in fond recollection.

"Yeah, my mom spent a lot of time in the kitchen too, making homemade pasta and cakes. When I awoke on a Sunday morning, I loved the aroma of her meatballs. She'd let me sample one as we readied for church."

Tony's face saddened. *Where did I go wrong? I had a solid upbringing, one of love and care. What made me change?*

The others left him to his introspection as they stepped into the adjoining kitchen garden and inhaled fragrant scents of herbs and flowers.

Mason said with passion, "Mothers are the core of love, the greatest gift to humanity, in fact co-creators with Our Majestic Father. You shall soon be graced to encounter the greatest of all Mothers, our sweet Mother of the Universe, the Queen of Peace and Love."

They discovered a section of the court where an older child was instructing children in the art of carpentry. The canopy above their heads consisted of tree branches, bonded with clay. In its time, it provided insulation from the desert sun as one worked. The happy children shaped wooden beams under the loving eyes of farm animals, which seemed to listen and give them encouragement.

"Hey, there are some of those singing logs like the ones we passed, and they're still glowing."

"Yes, Tony," Mason agreed. "As I said, God has a purpose for everything." Cornelael placed his hand over his heart in confirmation.

As Mason concluded his rundown, the young instructor, a boy of around twelve, welcomed them. "Shalom," he greeted them, with a fond lift to his voice. Mason and Corneal bowed in return.

"Come follow me," he said, with a whimsical smile and a mysterious sparkle to his eyes that penetrated their hearts. "Our Mother awaits you. She is weaving on the roof."

He led them up a sturdy wooden ladder, an outside stairway of sort, to the top. The expanse created an outdoor room that was shaded by a wood-framed trellis covered with shimmering lambskins. Obe and Tony fixed their eyes on each other, taking in the abundant aroma of roses, and they felt a strong flow of joyful energy in every pore of their skin.

The boy's mother sat at a loom. She rose to greet them—a woman of medium height, around five-foot-five. She wore a humble light gray tunic, and her head was covered in a white veil adorned with a faint halo of twelve golden stars. Tony and Obe froze in mid-step, mesmerized at the sight of her otherworldly beauty.

Mason and Cornelael knelt, unable to contain the awe and happiness they felt at her imposing presence. Glowing with love, she motioned them to their feet for a motherly embrace. She also extended her hands to Obe and Tony, directing bursts of energy to them, which cast them into a euphoric state of joy.

"Please sit," the boy said. He pointed to lambskin cushions on the floor while his mother assumed her position at the loom.

"Mother," he said with his hands palm up to her, "the children are in need of me. They are building a staircase, in answer to prayers of the faithful, in Our Earth's realm."

She bowed her head toward him and, with an extraordinary look of love in her violet colored eyes, she said, "Of course, my blessed love."

"Who is she?" Tony asked Obe softly.

"I believe she is the Mother of the Universe, Blessed Mary, Mother of Jesus, and Mother of us all."

"You're telling me that this stunning eighteen, maybe twenty-year-old, is the Blessed Virgin Mary?"

Mason nudged them to be still, and they watched the smiling young woman, who had begun to weave. As she did, balls of thread levitated from a table, assumed mid-air positions, and rotated around the loom as if in planetary orbit. The balls emitted a multitude of colorful lights that exuded energy from their core.

Now the young woman spoke to them. Her voice amplified and resounded through all their senses.

"My dear children, I am joyful in your company, for God Our Divine Father has graced you with the opportunity for the redemption of your souls and those of..." She stopped for a moment, sighing at the gravity of the task. "Soon His merciful love will knock harder upon the doors of your hearts. But will you answer the summons?"

Obe and Tony listened more intently, baffled by her question. At the same time, Cornelael and Mason put their arms around them in support, leaving no doubt as to whom the Mother was addressing her words.

"At the tender age of fourteen, I was asked by a messenger of God to birth His Son, who would rescue the world from sin. I answered yes, knowing I would sustain the greatest of sorrows for a mother to witness. It broke my heart to witness My Son's prophesized pain, anguish, and tortured death; to see Him humiliated by the dark power that distorts the judgment and will of God's creatures."

The four began to weep at her words, which also conveyed an internal vision of her despair--a mental picture of her as she knelt witnessing her Son's crucifixion. Their cascading red teardrops had a texture of mercury that caused a burning sensation as they lingered on their cheeks.

Her voice broke the solemnity of the moment. She asked them to look at her hands as she touched the threads attached to the orbiting balls of yarn.

"See how my children call out to me. How their souls yearn for peace and eternal life."

Her words brought flashes of images, of people and other creatures that sought her intercession with God. They saw how she appeared simultaneously at the same time to many: consoling, warning, teaching, and delivering a message that advocated for prayer. "The only remedy for the trials and tribulations that besets the world is prayer."

The images faded as she left her body at the loom, still weaving, healing, and consoling the world. Cornelael cracked a smile and was about to laugh, guessing the reactions the two were about to have to her bi-location, but she playfully admonished him with a motherly smile and a wave of her index finger.

"Come share my joy with our young builders below."

She seemed to glide down the ladder, and they all obediently followed, although with less agility.

She stopped at the workstation. "See the harvest of God's love. These are our cherished little souls who were denied the completion of their God-given earthly journeys."

Tony smiled with admiration at the children, who were busy constructing an intricate staircase, and marveled at their skill, precision, and how perfectly constructed it was.

"Casualties of war and famine. Their souls now experience the joy of self-realization; they learn and explore their talents, embellished now by our loving Father. And made active through my Son, who revels at their accomplishments."

Her eyes found Tony, who was taking it all in. "Praise is to the Triune God for you, Anthony Romero. You may wonder what purpose Heaven would have for a perfectly crafted stairwell? Well, actually, they have decided to bestow it as a gift, an answer to prayer for a faithful Earthly church community. One in dire need of one."

"Yes, Dear Mother," Tony said, not knowing if he should have spoken at all.

"I remember reading an article about something like that. A nun recited a nine-day novena to have a stairway somehow built in an impossible spot, in a very poor village church. Miraculously, on the last day of the novena, a carpenter showed up with tools and asked for work. He built it in a way that defied architectural reason, then left as mysteriously as he had arrived."

Cornelael and Mason laughed as the Blessed Mother confessed, "I guess you found us out."

Obe, confused, tried to add things up, and questioned with his penchant for reason, "But only one carpenter did the job. There are so many workers here."

She explained, "Actually, it was thought that it was my devoted husband Joseph, my earthly protector who accomplished the work. But he petitioned our Son after having heard faithful prayers, and thusly He assigned it to the children. They will draw lots to see who will take human form as the actual builder, who will be sent to the parishioners gifted with the combined skills of all the children."

Now with greater seriousness, she raised her hand to Obe and Tony and sent them both jolts of energy. Her eyes fixed on theirs, bestowing a blessing.

She asked them, "May our beloved Father of All Creations grace you with His Divine Mercy for the wisdom to harness your wills, in unconditional acceptance of that of His, and to be His instruments for building a new staircase to glory?"

Tony and Obe were filled with a deeper level of confidence.

Suddenly their eyes widened at the subtle sound of music that now filtered in. Cornelael announced its title. "The Battle Hymn of the Republic. Her favorite song."

Obe and Tony stood, illuminated with great love and admiration, as she prepared to depart.

"I leave for the Throne now. Be at peace as you conclude your journey. My prayers are with you always."

A swirling wind overtook them in a great spiral, and in a heartbeat they found themselves seated in comfort on the gilded coach, back in their tunics and without the need of a shave.

"That was beautiful," Mason said, tingling with excitement. "If you'd like, we can meditate and rest in the Spirit as we go on our path to further enlightenment in Throne City," he offered.

"I am speechless," Tony breathed. "The feelings...the feelings of being in Her presence are inexplicable. The closest I can describe it would be the times my mom held me as I fell asleep. I felt warm, safe, secure, and most of all, loved. Yet, in the presence of Our Lady I felt a million more times that."

"Bingo," Tony whispered to Obe. With outstretched hands, he added, "Obe, do you realize that we not only met the Blessed Virgin, but Jesus too...the twelve-year-old?"

"Oh yes. How I could have not surmised that?" Obe asked with an astonished look.

"Yes, I guess you're right." Tony shook his head in wonderment. "Goodness, He tugged at my tunic as He introduced us..."

"Well, if that's not a sign... tugging." Obe smirked. Then he poked Tony. "Please give it up already, will ya?"

Mason and Cornelael's faces read affirmation, as the coach ambled on and they drifted into a meditative state.

Twenty-eight

TONY CAME TO WAKEFULNESS from the sounds of harmonic bells and unusual chattering. His eyes opened to the presence of pudgy little angels the size of toddlers, with wings that fluttered with the speed of humming birds. Their movements exposed chubby bottoms clothed with golden loincloths, fastened with clips of precious jewels.

Soon all awakened to the prattle of these magical miniatures, who became more and more spirited as they perched themselves around and atop each of them. Each had a sun-kissed, cheery face, and great affection exuded from them all.

Mason, with childlike excitement, was the first to acknowledge them. "Greetings, magnificent progeny of God's love!" he said with joy. Then he tickled their bellies, prompting them to giggle. Their joyful reactions inebriated the four pilgrims with euphoric laughter.

Obe studied them, taken in wonder, and quietly asked Tony, "Do you notice how they glow, with these pulses of energy?"

"Yeah, everything and everyone glows here. But these little fellows seem to have a richer radiance. If you noticed, Cornelael shares it, and to some degree Mason shows patches of it too," Tony replied, returning affectionate caresses to the pint-sized creatures upon him.

"Yes, I have also noticed that on Mason," Obe remarked, and took a closer look at the tiny head rested upon his chest. "I think it happens to us to some degree when we wake from resting in the Spirit. Come to think of it, I've seen minute particles of similar brilliance upon you."

Tony saw that Mason was listening for his interpretation. But Cornelael responded for him.

"Oh, my loving brothers, God's wonders will never cease to amaze!" he blurted with a roar of laughter.

Mason touched the golden spots on his skin and explained.

"You may not have noticed, with the newness of it all for you, that many citizens here have varying degrees of this extraordinary brilliance."

He went on to explain. "The more souls rest in the Spirit, the more engrossed they become in a deeper communion. Many souls prefer this spiritual state; although still very much conscious and aware of the physical state of heaven, they choose to stay in the embrace of the Spirit, glorifying God. They are ultimately content, cradled in His essence of perfect peace and harmony. This is reflected when the soul chooses to return in physical form, and thusly displays this increased brilliance."

Obe interrupted, "Kind teacher, does that mean we will lose our individual identities?"

Tony ripped him a look. "Here we go again."

Mason raised his hand to quiet Tony and said, "Brother Obe, our wills are as permanent as Triune God's eternal love. He lives in us and we live in him, manifested by the incarnation of Our Divine Lord and Brother Jesus. Moreover, through the presence of the Holy Spirit, who is the Eternal Love of the Father and the Son—the Gift of God. He is the Creator Spirit, present before the existence of the universe, and through His power, God the Father made everything in Christ."

Mason stopped for a moment, peered deeply into Obe's eyes, and recognized he had given him a textbook answer. He shook his head at himself, and summed it up a different way.

"Dear Brother, it is not that we lose identity, but in fact gain it, like never before."

This is deep, Tony thought. Then, unable to resist, he zinged Obe. "Can you fathom it, Obe? God wants to give us everything, and you're still looking to pick an apple from the wrong tree."

Obe spat back with an edge to his voice, "Judge not, lest you be judged."

Feeling the growing tension, the miniature creatures fell silent. Mason interrupted to avoid further confrontation. "You are both still developing and remain at an orientation level, with God's purpose still undisclosed. Continue to contemplate what you hear and experience. Abide the Holy Spirit's work in it."

Mason underscored his remarks with a finger pointed to the red spots on their tunics. He concluded his instruction with a grin and a warning.

"Admonishments will only give you a return trip to the dark side of your moon," he chuckled.

Cornelael laughed heartedly at his words, bringing smiles to Obe and Tony. The cherubs resumed their addictive playfulness and, with a few more affectionate hugs, they flew to follow groups of angels headed in the direction of the golden horizon.

"Cornelael, devoted defender and servant of the Most High, you seem to take great joy in the reactions we have to what surprises us."

"Oh yes, very much so, Brother Obe." He blushed with a mischievous expression. "I take great pleasure in knowing what wonders may ultimately be awarded to both you and Brother Tony." In a warm gesture, he placed his hands on them and offered further explanation, "It's like knowing what to expect when one dear to you is about to open a present that you know will thrill him to no end."

Before long, they found themselves in front of a massive archway made of brilliant white pearl. Implanted at its crest were the symbols of the alpha and omega.

The coach stopped, and two enormous angels presented themselves with ceremonial bows. This pair dwarfed Cornelael's nine-foot frame, and wore large pearl breastplates also embossed with the sign of the Alpha and Omega. Without a spoken word, they directed the riders to disembark.

"These guys," Tony says, "have a stark seriousness about them, like they are Secret Service agents guarding a President."

Obe studied them, flicking his eyes back to Cornelael to measure his nine-foot height against theirs, which seemed to double his. "Yes, quite impressive. The size of church pillars. They seem to have an ancient aura about them, as if they have lived forever."

Tony and Obe instantly felt a special quiet inside them, emptied of all concerns. One of the statue-like hosts motioned them through the arch and onto a short path, which brought them to the shoreline of a scintillating, slow-moving river. At the water's edge were giant lily pads.

Wordlessly, the angels invited them to step up onto a lush green pad, which immediately produced a large flower whose petals formed into a bench for them to seat themselves.

Tony's eyes rolled in amazement. "You know," he started to say, but then stopped and shook his head, taking a moment to come to terms with the wonder of it all. "You know, if Webster is here he must be going crazy trying to develop words that can truly describe all of this."

Obe nodded. "Imagine the artists, the painters; oh, the colors must have baffled their senses upon their arrival here."

Mason and Cornelael smiled as the Angel gently launched the pad in the direction of the golden horizon.

The living raft softly drifted while species of exotic fish with different shapes and colors surfaced, awarding the pad's occupants endearing gazes.

Then all at once, a blue-skinned, seal-like mammal startled them as he catapulted himself upon the pad in a big splash. His large crystalline eyes and smile reflected intense love as he introduced himself.

"Blessed children of He who Is and always will Be. Welcome to the river of the One, the tributary to the one universal destination. I am Moratael, a Sea Angel, from the choir of Aquatic Angels that patrol the seas of the universe, doing the will of Our Father."

Obe and Tony looked upon him with stupefied faces. Curiously, for them, not only did the impromptu visitor speak, but he also spoke like an Oxford scholar.

Moratael, with a theatric flair similar to that of Cornelael, elucidated, "You know, someone had to aid Our Lord in gathering those fish for Blessed Peter and the other Apostles." He roared with laughter. Naturally, Cornelael joined him with gusto.

Moratael spun with enthusiasm and raised his fin. "See what awaits you."

What unfolded before their eyes, in the midst of the golden horizon, was a spectacular jeweled city that brought gasps and gulps at its beauty.

"I have seen this many times before, yet it always stirs me as if it were the first," Mason shared with a deep sigh.

Seeing that his audience was engrossed by what they saw, the seal propped up on his tail fin to gain their attention once more. "Oh, yes, the sweetest of all visions, I must say."

He twisted once more and pointed to an island covered by cherry trees in full bloom. In that instant, the pad beached upon its shore and moored itself in the crystal sand.

When they stepped off the pad, Moratael transformed into a mostly-traditional angelic form, with blonde hair and a round face. However, his skin was tinted in iridescent turquoise. His down-feathered wings, though, were stark white.

He adjusted his blue tunic, which draped off one shoulder to expose the presence of a gill. Obe and Tony's eyes grew wide at the sight of the gill upon his exposed side.

Moratael noticed their curiosity and laughed. He then comically offered, "You know, you can take a boy out of the ocean, but you can't take the ocean out of the boy." This brought more laughter from the group, especially Cornelael; this kind of humor was right up his alley.

Without delay, their guide led them down a shiny brick path through a spectacular cherry tree grove, where flowers lit up the trees with vibrant colors.

Obe tugged on Tony's tunic. "You know Brother, as we sailed on that pad I had a yen for sweets."

"Yeah, me too. Those cherries look pretty good, don't they?"

No sooner had he said this than large, luscious cherries of every variety began to fall into their hands. They wasted no time and bit into their crisp fullness, which released sweet nectar. Captivated by the exquisite taste, and overwhelmed with pleasure, their eyes searched each other's in wonder. They could not find adequate words to describe the special flavor and sweetness of the fruit.

In his exuberance, and unable to resist, Cornelael tossed a robust cherry at Moratael, who paddled a return swing with the back of his wing. This opening salvo provoked an all-out cherry fight between them all.

After bouncing a juicy one off Cornelael's forehead, Mason raised his hands in submission. "Okay now, let's calm down and regain our composure," he laughed. Waving them on, he said with keen interest, "I smell the aroma of something baking up ahead."

They took in the beauty of the island as they ambled along, and soon they came to a clearing, where they found a contingent of Sea Angels in chef hats. Approaching closer, they saw the angels remove fresh-baked cherry pies from an enormous oven made of the same gleaming brick as the path. The air was filled with fragrant aroma as the celestial bakers welcomed them with bows.

Moratael invited them to sit at a dining table set for five. The table was exquisite, supporting bowls of fresh whipped cream and golden-crusted cherry pies shaped like fish. Cups of piping hot coffee were set at each place setting.

The congenial Sea Angel placed his hands together prayerfully, and the others followed.

"Let us give thanks and praise to our Eternal Father for His many gifts, not the least of which is the surprise of our creation and eternal life." He ended with a deep reverent bow and continued, "My brothers, enjoy this sweet gift of profound love in its simplicity."

As they took their first bites and sips of coffee, Moratael extended his arm in welcome to a young man, in his thirties, who approached the table. He was dressed in a white linen tunic, and his handsome face shone with tranquility under a crop of jet-black hair. His blue eyes were warm and kind; all in all, a very fetching presence.

Moratael invited the man to sit at the head of the table, in front of a wedge of pie platted on a fish-shaped dish and a gold cup of fresh coffee.

Moratael, coffee cup in hand, toasted, "Obe, Tony, praise is to the Triune God for you. May He grant you the courage to accept His love, will, mercy, and the Gift of life eternal." That said, he shot them bursts of energy, and he and the other sea angels dematerialized in a glistening mist.

Tony spoke first. "What a delightful soul, Mason--full of joy, and funny too."

"Love binds us all, Tony. Each unique, yet all one."

The man at the head of the table nodded in agreement and introduced himself as Riccardo Gutierrez. He explained that he fared from Madrid, Spain, born to a wealthy industrialist family. He went on to say that he had accepted the call at an early age to become a Catholic priest. Soon after, he received an offer, through the graces of the church fathers, for the opportunity to study psychology, and eventually received his doctorate. His first assignment placed him at the Vatican Congregation for Catholic Education. Later, around the time of his passing, he had served as an exorcist.

"By the Mercy of God I only just arrived here myself. My story is not much different than both of yours." He nodded directly to both Tony and Obe. "I might add that, under tragic circumstances, I also gave my life for other souls."

He shrugged and picked up his fork. "However, enough of me right now. Enjoy your pie and coffee with your companions, who are soon to take leave of you."

Obe and Tony's eyebrows rose in surprise.

"You know, cherry pie is one of God's favorites. He likes pizza too, mushroom to be exact," he finished with a playful smile. Then he stood and walked away in order to give them time for a goodbye.

Mason and Cornelael searched Obe and Tony's faces with eyes of parental love.

Tony broke the silence, his face shocked and sad. "You're leaving us?"

Mason choked a reply, "I just became aware this moment. Worry not, Cornelael and I will continue to be with you in a different way. Your deep love for our Creator has added to our joy, and we look forward to our continued journey through eternity together. For now, you will continue to reside in our hearts."

They all rose in parting. Cornelael took them both under his wings for a moment. When he released them, he addressed Obe first.

"My dear brother Obe, praise is to God for you, for your love and your unshakeable belief. But know, my dear brother that a gift, to be a *gift*, must be accepted."

Making eye contact with Tony, he said, "Tony Romero, my brother, praise is to God for you, for your love and your courage." He pointed to the gold watch on Tony's wrist, the one he had given him, the one with no hands. "Brother, remember me in time," he chuckled. "All of us here in the heavenly realms are counting on you to honor our Lord, but no pressure," he ended with a laugh.

As Mason and Cornelael made their way down the path in the direction of the shoreline, Obe bolted to them and gripped Mason Pringle's hands.

"My dear professor, will I make it? Will I be lost?" He took a breath. "Thank you for all you have done. What you taught me, and for the love even my parents had not shown me."

"Oh, my dear brother, with the love you have for the Almighty and with the honesty you have shown Him about your feelings, even though sustaining the pains of Paraclete City, I am sure He has purpose for you. Remember, His mercy is infinite. The real question is if you will accept it. For now, go, and trust in Him."

Twenty-nine

TONY GAZED AT OBE WITH SADNESS as he rejoined him at the table. He empathized with Obe's feelings and respected his courage to stand up for what he believed, even if it was against the Almighty Himself. Nevertheless, his empathy changed into more frustration and doubt as to Obe's ability to see past his anger and accept God's will.

All the signs that they had received together came to mind, especially the wonderful souls they had met and the guidance of Mason and Cornelael, not to mention the glorious sight of Jesus and His Blessed Mother. Tony cried within, *Obe please give it up.*

Tony did a quick personal inventory, and became profoundly aware of his own lack of faithfulness in the selfish life he had led. He compared himself to Obe, who he respected for his strong faith and the love he had for God, which made him feel even more unworthy. Tony tried to understand what ultimate purpose God had for them. Somehow, he knew deep in his soul that something monumental was about to happen.

Both sat as if frozen in time, trying to adjust to the separation from their celestial friends Mason and Cornelael. Tony whispered, "Why?" He then sent up a silent appeal: *The entire populace of heaven carries the red stain because of us...insignificant us. Why?*

As if he had read his thoughts, Obe placed his hand on Tony's shoulder and attempted to comfort him. In a sorrowful tone, he said, "It's not you Tony. It's me. I am the dissenter and the cause of this schism."

Then, as if he had heard all of Tony's inner thoughts, Obe gave out a deep-gut howl, and lamented, "Why?" He repeated it twice more, "Why? Why?"

Tony grasped Obe's hand in firm reassurance. "For what it's worth, I'm here and I care about you. I know I am less worthy than you to be here; it's a gift that still confounds me."

Obe placed his free hand atop Tony's and spoke with his head down. "You are the only real friend I ever had. I am grateful for that, but I will not let you lose your place here. So let me do the arguing with God." He said this last with an effort at comic relief, in an attempt to calm his friend's tormented thoughts.

"Be at peace, my brothers," Riccardo quietly advised them. There was joy in his voice. "Our Lord and Divine Brother Jesus, through His infinite mercy, will win favor for you with the Great I AM."

The priest peered at them closely and asked a surprising question: "Will you sacrifice and bear the pains of His passion once again?"

At this, both Tony and Obe stirred in their seats. Tony shot Obe an *I told you so* look.

Obe asked sharply, "How can He choose me for anything, with this disagreement we have?"

A large rumble of thunder, accompanied by the vibration of the table, interrupted their heated discourse. Fearful and frustrated, Tony reached out and squeezed Obe's arm.

"What is wrong with you? You still have no idea where we are and who you are dealing with? This is insane!" He looked at Riccardo with his lips pressed together. "I think that description captures it."

Riccardo broke the strained moment. "Speaking about insanity," he chuckled, "let me tell you about my own crazy self."

Riccardo shared how his own dysfunction had blocked his ability to accept himself. He explained that for most of his human life he had not had self-respect. Certainly he had been successful on the exterior, but under his outward persona had dwelled a self-condemning attitude. He had felt unloved, and had blamed himself for everything, a mindset that had short-circuited his ability to learn to love God.

"In therapy, I came to the conscious realization, with some reluctance, that the unintentional emotional mistreatment wielded by my parents in my youth affected how I saw the world, God, and myself."

Obe's and Tony's faces tightened, making it apparent to Riccardo that his words touched something in them.

Riccardo pounded his fist on the table, which really got their attention. "I denied the resentment I had of them. I asked myself how two well-meaning souls, ones that I loved so much, could be capable of such abuse. Nevertheless, when I addressed the submerged pain, I came to terms with the fact that they were frightened of the world. Because of that, they became demeaning, judgmental, and overbearing to me. I saw it as an attempt to control me, in order to shield me from the hardness of life and their having to deal with it in some way."

He further revealed that he had also had difficulty with those in authority: bosses, teachers, etc., throughout his life. In defense, he had developed a certain craftiness in order to deal with situations of instability. He taught himself to manage arbitrary authority figures who had power over his future.

He peered at Tony, "You know. You're from New York. 'Street wise'."

Tony nodded.

"In principle, I had become selfish and emotionally blocked. Although I believed in God, I did not have the ability to appreciate His love for us." With his hand upon his heart he asked, "How could I? I did not love myself."

Tony cut in, "You know, I became aware of my selfish attitude when Pinchot sat me on the pedestal of introspection to review my life. In my case, my parents were very good to me. They spoiled me maybe too much. I felt entitled."

Thinking some more, Tony shared, "I knew that both sets of my grandparents were hard on my Mom and Dad; from what my folks had told me and led me to believe, they were, at times, somewhat cruel." This was behavior Tony had attributed to the pressure of their being immigrants in a strange country, with different customs, obstructed by prejudice, and not least, the plight of the Depression.

Obe, touched by what he heard, began to cry with regret. His tears drenched the red stain on his tunic. Tony reached out to him, but Riccardo signaled to allow him to let it out.

Tony marveled at the sight of Obe's tears. They turned into diamond-shaped crystals and fell into Obe's lap. *Oh my God,* he said to himself, *even tears are wondrous in Heaven.*

When Obe regained control, he revealed for the first time ever that his father had dealt with him in a strong, seemingly arbitrary fashion. He confessed that the man was a strict fundamentalist, one who imposed severe punishment for normal childhood infractions.

"You know," he told them, "at age eight, I left a lamb out in the pasture overnight. My father became so angry that he took me to the woodshed and applied ten lashes of his belt upon my bottom. Then he had me spend an afeared night alone in the dark pasture, with sounds of wolves in the vicinity and in fear of a prowling mountain lion." Obe whirled his fist into the air and went on, "I had to be perfect; had to carry a heavy work burden, never question or show my irritation, and read my Bible whether I wanted to or not, etc."

Tony cautioned him to take it easy, but Obe was in full flight. He choked on his words but went on, "My father hardly spoke to me, other than giving instructions or direction to do chores. Even when we spent a day in the woods hunting. Not one word would pass between us."

Tony stood to pour cups of coffee, and his hand quivered as he did. *I guess this may be where the problem lies,* he mused.

He sat back down and Riccardo resumed.

"Through my therapy, prayer, and formation at the seminary I came to believe that true love came from divine love, which requires us to love ourselves and our fellow man to acquire it."

Riccardo's face shone even more as he continued to describe his conversion experience. "In order to love ourselves, we needed to cease from self-condemnation and truly believe that God does not want to slam us. Proof of that clearly lies in the gospels, where in many instances He spoke of His desire for our salvation."

Riccardo rose and stretched his hands above Obe's head, symbolic of dispensing a healing prayer.

"My brother," he said, "loving ourselves means that we have to stop blaming ourselves for past failures. The sins and evils we employed in the past, and the feelings of doubt or antipathy that we harbor within, can have no impact or deter us from God's grace and infinite mercy, if we trust in Him. We cannot experience love without loving God, who in His nature Is love, and the Source of all love."

Riccardo's words appeared to have an influence on Obe and Tony. Obe stopped playing with the remnants of his cherry pie, and Tony ceased stirring his coffee. Both froze in contemplation.

Riccardo described more of his personal revelations. He confessed that he had chastised himself for falling short of perfection. Even though he had said Mass every day and had expounded in his homilies about God's unceasing love, and had taught on how we should trust in Him, inside he had not believed it possible for himself.

"At first, I believed the priesthood attracted me because of my emotional disorder. Obedience came easy to me. However, following orders was more an act of spite rather than love. It served as a psychological defense against my unconscious rage. It was an 'I'll show you.'"

He had challenged himself in therapy, and had come to terms with his discontent and self-doubt. He had eventually accepted that his attitude was an emotional defense, one subconsciously contrived to hurt his parents, who had failed him and left him to feel unloved.

Tony interrupted once again. "Yes, I can relate to that," he said. "I did some mean things. As a kid, I would break my cousin's toys on purpose, or rip his comic books. Later on, in business, I did treacherous things to my competitors. I can see now that I also had that inner irritation you speak of, but my antagonism came from a false sense of entitlement. I thirsted for more and more. It was about me, only me."

Obe shook his head with remorse and confided, "I just realized why I challenged and disrespected the Pastor at Sunday service. I know now--it served to hurt my father, who was fanatically protective of the church. Nothing stopped me though, even knowing that I'd take a licking for it."

Riccardo sipped some coffee, then changed the subject to lessen the tension. "This coffee is fabulous. You know, it's the special blend of St. Pedro Claver, a Jesuit priest and one of the patron saints of Colombia, a country known worldwide for its robust coffee. The Saint worked to convert many souls to Christianity and to abolish the slave trade. Colombia, though famous for coffee, also had an infamous reputation for being a center for slave distribution."

He smiled and went on with his story. "I came to terms with my desire to hurt others, specifically my father, who was the authority in our home. I had condemned him for his lack of guidance, protection, or emotional involvement. I realized that this detachment hindered him from feeling love, giving love, and most of all from really loving God, Who he worshipped legalistically."

He took another moment, then added with remorse in his voice, "Without love there can be no forgiveness, and without forgiveness there can be no love. My dysfunctional defense, one of perfectionism, caused an unfortunate effect. I hurt others in my life. Mostly those who, in my pride, I judged fell short of deserving it."

Obe rose to his feet and circled the table, weighted with introspection. His tumbling crystal tears fell in a trail behind him.

Tony asked with curiosity, "You said you arrived there, Purgatory, under similar circumstances--saving the life of another?"

"Yes." Riccardo recounted that he had gone out for a late dinner on a balmy summer night, to a family restaurant on a quiet street near his quarters at the Vatican in Rome. After dinner, he had exited the restaurant and had come upon a man out front, in the midst of robbing two female tourists at gunpoint.

Riccardo's instinct had placed him between the gunman and the women. He had shielded them and shouted for them to run to safety. Turning back, he had told the robber that he was a priest, in the hope that it would deter the man. But the robber had become enraged at his interference, and without second thought had fatally shot him.

Tony closed his eyes in sadness. "You and Obe are the true heroes. What I did was on an unconscious level. There was no gun pointed at me. I did not have fear for my life."

Riccardo laughed. "Didn't you hear what I said about self-doubt?" He then cackled again. Tony, embarrassed, tilted his head down and smiled.

Obe stopped in his tracks. "Brother Riccardo," he asked with fury, "did you forgive the man that murdered you?"

"Yes. Most definitely yes. At the very moment the bullets entered my body, I offered prayers for his soul, even as life drained from me."

"Do you think that he should be sent to hell for eternity, should he not repent? And for that matter should all the fallen souls, already there in Hell, be doomed forever?" Obe asked obstinately, still seeking a supporter for his cause.

Tony kicked the table. "Again? Will you never stop this insanity? Will you?" He threw his hands up in the air in frustration.

Riccardo gently motioned for Tony to calm down, and provided a response to Obe's questions.

"Brother, my heart, and I'm sure the hearts of all good souls, find it very disconcerting that any soul be lost. I imagine how God must feel as the Divine Parent, one whose every intention is to give each every one of His children royal status in His kingdom.

"One who offered His Only Begotten Son in sacrifice for the redemption of all souls. Crucified for us in His infinite Mercy in an act to shield humanity from total separation from God. To me, it is no different from parents who want the best for their children. Who, out of unconditional love, show them forgiveness for their many grievous imperfections."

Obe nodded in affirmation, but still questioned, "Kind Brother, with my whole heart I believe that God is loving and merciful. I also know that His intentions for us are beautiful and good. He shows infinite mercy and forgiveness, but why can He not alter the hearts of the fallen? Is it not painful for Him to see their eternal suffering? However self-imposed it may be?"

Tony twisted a cloth napkin as if he were wringing someone's neck, and leaned over the table to Riccardo. "I have a question too, brother. How is it that insanity is permitted to exist here in heaven?" He asked it with a dark stare at Obe.

Obe raised his brows and poised to return a verbal assault, but he was interrupted.

All at once, they heard a rumble and felt a vibration under their feet. In an instant, they beheld the immediate appearance of defender Angels. They stood before them dressed in battle regalia, brandishing swords as they did before.

Tony calmed himself with haste. "Please, most gracious brothers," he pleaded, with his hands together as if in prayer, fearing that they may hurl them both back to the dark side of the moon.

The Archangel Gabriel stepped forward to address them, "My dear brothers, praise is to He who Is and always will Be for you. Be at peace, for He has shown great favor upon you. Let His Divine Plan unfold with trust." He said this with a knowing smile and stepped back.

Riccardo exploded with laughter. "You two remind mind me of those great Hollywood comedians, Abbott and Costello, who were a great source of entertainment for me in my youth. Their humor was derived from an uneven relationship between two partners, with different personalities and behavior."

Tony, now very calm, laughed. "Yeah, I remember watching their TV reruns." He looked at Obe with a forgiving smile. "They were really funny, Obe."

Unanticipated, a large ancient Roman-like boat, illuminated in a golden mist and ornately decorated with carvings of angels, descended from the sky. Its Angel occupants were singing the Battle Hymn of the Republic while, without much effort, they churned the vessel's many oars. The Archangel Gabriel ushered them aboard, followed by the contingent of his defender Angels.

On deck now, Obe declared, "I know that song. The Negro slaves sang it all the time."

"Yes," Gabriel answered, "it has inspired great faith in Our Lord and it is a favorite of Our Divine Mother, Blessed Mary, Queen of Heaven."

Thirty

THE SAILS DROPPED FROM THE VESSEL'S three masts and a robust breeze filled them, launching it skyward. Obe, Tony, and Riccardo sat on red-cushioned couches that embraced them in soft comfort. Riccardo announced that they were taking another interim trip. Surprised, Tony asked, "I thought we were to enter Throne City?

Obe threw Riccardo an inquisitive look too.

"Yes we are, but the Holy Spirit suggested another exercise of introspection on our way. "

Obe opened his mouth to question the plan, but with a glance at Tony thought better of it.

As the flying boat began to sail, a holographic display appeared before them.

Tony was once again overwhelmed, and he remarked, "You travel around here like in Disneyland!"

Obe, confused by the term, questioned, "What?"

Riccardo explained, "It's an amusement park, where people embark on different means of transport to view entertaining displays, often accompanied by festive music."

Obe smiled at Tony's humor.

The holograph totally immersed them. They became spectators of a lecture at Seminary in Hippo back around AD 400. In attendance that day were a number of bishops, priests, seminarians, deacons, and Doctors of the Church. Unbeknown to the observers, they were about to hear a reading of St. Augustine's dogmatic treatment of The Fall of Lucifer.

The architectural design of the lecture hall was modeled on that of the Roman Senate. At the podium was the great Church scholar himself, Augustine, the Bishop of Hippo. He nodded to a seminarian, positioned at another podium, to read aloud his examination of the 'fall', the original schism at the time of creation.

He signaled, and the student nodded and began reading the Saint's words with trained formality:

"God, in the beginning, had created together two creatures, the spiritual and the corporeal, that is to say the angelic and the earthly. Man was made of both spirit and body. The angels, before their fall, had received a revelation of the future incarnation of the Son of God (Jesus) and in consequence, the angels had to adore Jesus as their God, the Son of Man, who was presented to them in human form.

He paused to hear any questions that those in the audience might offer. The visitors just sat trying to digest the depth of what they had heard, so he continued:

"To Lucifer, the most powerful of all angels and second only to God, it was a great humiliation for the angels, who had to acknowledge that in spite of their sublime natural perfections they had no claim to the divine son-ship."

As the young seminarian paused again, Tony offered his opinion with conviction, "It's obvious--jealousy and envy."

Riccardo flashed him a thumbs-up. "Amazing, isn't it. Lucifer, by nature, was the most magnificent of all God's creatures and second only to God."

Obe did not speak, but his face reflected introspection.

As before, the speaker's eyes searched the audience for comments. Hearing none, he resumed.

"Then Lucifer, also referred to as Satan, and angels of lesser stature, also known as demons, chose to rebel against God, causing a Schism, there be it the Fall. Although God created them good in their nature, they, by themselves, made themselves evil because of sinful pride."

He surveyed the participants and read from their faces that the complex material needed time for digestion in its entirety, so without further delay he began the final paragraph:

"The power of Satan is, nonetheless, not infinite. He is only a creature, powerful from the fact that he is pure spirit, but still a creature. He cannot prevent the building up of God's reign. Although Satan may act in the world out of hatred for God and His kingdom in Christ Jesus, and although his action may cause grave injuries - of a spiritual nature, and indirectly, even of a physical nature - to each man and to society, the action is permitted by Divine Providence, which with strength and gentleness guides human and cosmic history."

He stopped for breath and went on to conclude with stronger emphasis, *"It is a great mystery that Providence should permit diabolical activity."* He paused to take another breath, trying to comprehend the profound words himself. *"But we know that in everything God works for good with those who love Him."*

Hearing the last two lines, Tony challenged Obe once again, "Did you hear that? This thing about going against

God has greater implications for sure, and way above our heads. That is why we need to trust in Him. Why fight God? He can throw you out of here too. You can wind up in the lowest level at Paraclete City for a long, long time, almost like being in Hell."

Riccardo quieted Tony once again as they drifted out of the Holograph. They watched as the flying boat descended and made a soft landing onto a sparkling river. The giant pads of the water plants moved aside to create a clear path, giving free passage toward the glow of Throne City now visible in the near distance.

Obe, still seething inside with Tony's comments and lingering thoughts of his implications, came back at him, "Tell me, Brother Tony, why He will not forgive those souls in Hell?

Tony flared back, "You jerk, they don't want to be forgiven!"

Just as he said it, he heard the threat of a rumble and cast down his eyes. "Sorry," he whispered, then asked Obe in a gentler voice, "Do you not see that?"

Tony collected his thoughts and continued, a little more stern this time, "It was their choice to make, as we just heard. Lucifer gave up his place in this kingdom out of pride. Imagine how God felt about that, rejected by a child of His that He had given everything to.

"I know you do not want power over God, as I have said before. You loved Him and accepted His existence from your childhood. You lived a faithful, hardworking life. You loved and respected your parents, even though they were hard on you, and in your final deed on Earth you sacrificed your life to save the life of a child.

"I am convinced that your stints in Levels One and Two were of your own making. You had an express ticket here and threw it away."

Tony scratched his head as he thought, and picked up again.

"By rights, I should have been there a much longer time. I wavered about God my whole life and did some horrendous things. If only I had allowed myself to learn to love Him more while on Earth, I'd feel more justified being here now."

Obe asked him, "You mean you did not choose Purgatory?"

Tony shook his head, astounded at the question. "What are you talking about? Of course not. Who in his right mind would?"

Seeing the sharpness on Obe's face, Tony clarified, "What I meant was, that for you it didn't have to happen, if only you had accepted His Will and trusted that He was on the job."

"I know, I know," Obe agreed with an edge to his voice. He then asked with curiosity, "When you sat on the pedestal of enlightenment, were you not given a choice to where you should go?"

"What are you talking about? I think you have really lost it." He shook his head with an impatient sigh.

"Nevertheless, may we take it, Tony," Riccardo interjected with a question of his own, "that you had not been asked to decide your own fate. Is that so? Each of us arriving at the pedestal are customarily asked where we want to go--Heaven, Purgatory, or Hell. Because at that point we have no human guile. We can only speak the truth and answer it so."

"Wow," Tony said with surprise. "No, I wasn't asked. I didn't know for sure where I was going until practically there at the banquet with Pinchot."

Riccardo probed further, his face reflecting disbelief. "You had a Banquet before you entered Purgatory?"

Obe spoke before he could answer. "Oh my God! Tony, that's why you were there for such a short time." With a knowing look he turned his eyes to Riccardo. "He's going back, isn't he?"

Riccardo just stared. Tony took it as an affirmative, causing him to ask aloud with a panicked gag, "Going back to Purgatory?"

Obe corrected with great seriousness, "No, you misunderstood. Not Purgatory, my brother. I think, back down to Earth."

Realizing the full implications of what he had just projected, Obe questioned inside, *My God, what have I just said? What is this all about?*

Their discussion was interrupted by the sound of the Helmsman's horn signaling a stop.

The boat slowed to dock. Tony moved to port side and spotted his guardian, Archangel Pinchot, standing on a marble pier decorated with streamers of vibrant red silk. Pinchot himself was dressed in his signature white tuxedo, also marked with a red stain upon his chest. He waved to them.

The oarsmen raised and secured their oars as the boat moored without a sound. An angel deck hand extended a golden gangway and welcomed Pinchot aboard. "Praise and Glory is to Our Almighty Father for you, our eternal brother," he heralded.

"Also to you and your devoted choir."

Tony rose to his feet, happy to greet him. "Praise to God is for you, my beloved Guardian."

"And to you, my heavenly charge," Pinchot replied, and zinged him with a burst of electric energy. After greeting the others in a similar fashion, they sat upon the cushioned couch.

Tony spoke first. "Pinchot, I was just thinking about you."

"I know. That's why I'm here."

"Where have you been?"

"Oh my dear brother, basking in the Divine Glory of Our Father and enjoying what you may call a 'vacation' with members of my Choir. In fact, I am delighted to report that I came in second place in our chess tournament. Considering the participants numbered a thousand, I am pleased with my effort." They all laughed and clapped at his victory.

Riccardo brought Pinchot up to speed on what they had deliberated. He gave the angel a synopsis of the informative holographic visit at St. Augustine's lecture, and utilized parts of a 'linger', similar to the one Tony experienced in the elevator at Paraclete City with Pinchot. After learning what they had experienced, Pinchot offered to participate.

"Brother Riccardo, may I provide some input to them about the state of angels?"

"Yes, of course, please. You were present there at the glorious time of creation. An eyewitness so to speak. What could be better?"

Pinchot settled in and began to explain the nature of the Angelic Will. "Angels, like man, are given free will, and by it we're able to choose to serve God or not. However, unlike man, we cannot waver back and forth, but rather see everything in an instant to its logical conclusion. Given that, if we decide to turn against God and His plan, it remains unchangeable and everlasting."

Tony and Obe gasped at the weight of his words.

"At the time of the Fall, many of the angels were cast at once into Hell. They had decided to follow Lucifer, one of prominence in the highest scale of the angels, in his rebellion against God. Since their wills were thusly set, freely accepting evil, their decision not to serve God in essence would disallow repentance."

Pinchot lowered his head in marked sadness before he continued, "What has always troubled me was the high level of malice in their sin, because they knew better. We Angels, through the infinite gift of the Almighty, have a greater capacity for understanding; confusion, ignorance, and weakness have no effect on us. Pure and simple, their fall from grace can only be attributed to their sinful pride."

Supported by Pinchot's words, Tony peered at Obe, who tensed and waited for another verbal sting.

It was not long in coming. "Brother, did you hear that? It was their choice, same as the choice made by the souls who occupy Hell. They bought into pride as the Devil did, and freely exercised their free will."

Obe's eyes rolled impatiently. He blew out a frustrated sigh as Tony continued, "I'm not saying that your so-called disagreement with God is as grave as their sinful pride, but for certain it is a disrespect of the highest order. You would think that after all we received from Him, not the least being the sorrowful passion of Jesus, and how He bestowed a magnitude of mercy and forgiveness on us, we still hesitate to trust in Him."

Tony stopped once again to read the expressions of the others, who he noticed had remained quiet. Obe just stared at him like a wounded animal overwhelmed by an injury.

Tony went on, "Obe, I believe you're at the point of making a similar decision, and long in coming I must say. I guess you need to ask yourself if you will choose for God. You and I both know that God will require a choice, not only for you but for me too. I feel it."

"Yes, I know that's coming," Obe said under his breath.

"Obe, I love you, and the thought of us not sharing the eternal adventure is quite disconcerting. In fact, I realize now how much I would miss even those others that I had disregarded on Earth. I see now how special and unique they all were. Please, Obe, search your soul."

Tony closed his eyes, marveling to himself, *Wow, I can't believe I said that.*

Riccardo and Pinchot read each other to see who would continue the dialogue. Riccardo took the lead. "You know, as I mentioned, flagrant dysfunction in a familial home can stain a child. Like me, children can grow with bitterness, which can cause oppositional and defiant behavior. In its extreme, it can paralyze a child's emotions, and even lead him into anti-social activity and a life of sin. Most often, though, emotional damage in "normal" families is from the authority figures that demonstrate arbitrary, unfair, or hypocritical conduct."

Obe nervously scratched at his chin again, searching for clarity with a look to Tony. Riccardo kept on describing what he had learned, with an eye of sympathy for Obe.

"It is unfortunate that parental figures are afflicted so, and use Church teaching as a weapon. So in effect, for their children, God becomes another foreboding presence in their lives. Another hammer about the head, if you will. Many parents hide behind the precepts of religion that they extol, but they themselves fail to act or honor its principals."

Riccardo concluded, "Children, those subjected to this emotional suffocation, grow and develop in an environment of manipulation, intimidation, and discouraged communication. This leaves them feeling frustrated, angry, and with a jaded opinion of God Who, in their subconscious mind, is the ultimate authority figure. Thusly, they apply their resistance to Him."

Both Tony and Obe nodded in the affirmative.

Pinchot also commented, "If I might add: sometimes ghostly spirits, because of this fear of authority, fail to take the path through the tunnel of light at the end of their mortal lives and are left to dwell between these two realities."

Obe asked, "Is that what happened to my traveling companion, Elijah Thompson?"

"Most likely, having suffered emotional and physical brutality by his slave masters, which were his authority figures," Pinchot answered.

With a tone of sadness, he continued, "And then there are others, those of evil nature, who do not enter the light for fear of damnation. Because of this, they roam the confines of the earth, left subject to the domination and manipulation of evil spirits, who utilize them in diabolical mischief. However, all can take the portal at any instant of their choosing."

The angels, as if they had been given silent instruction, lowered their oars, and Riccardo announced, "It is time. Let us meditate and rest in the spirit, and discover our greater purpose as our journey continues." There was a tone of mystery to his voice, which intrigued Tony and Obe.

Tony, from habit, checked his watch. Seeing the dial with no hands, he smiled. *Fooled once again.*

Thirty-one

FOR OBE, THIS MEDITATION FELT different from those he had experienced before. Now he found himself in a dream-like state, in which he viewed an inventory of sorts. It was a recounting of all he had learned on his celestial journey with Tony, and the experiences they had had with the other souls along the way. The most prominent was his most recent time with Riccardo, and his assessment of the evil of dysfunction brought about by childhood trauma.

In this dream, Obe began to soften. He had become more agreeable to take some, but not all, responsibility for his contrary behavior. However, there was a sizable part of it still frozen in disagreement.

In a moment, he arrived atop the crest of a hill, which was blanketed with light like none he had ever seen on Earth or in Paradise thus far. The expanse that spread out before his eyes astounded him. He placed both hands on his head as he gazed upon this monument of radiant beauty. The valley beneath unfolded with countless acres of what he thought to be brilliant flowers, illuminated in dazzling gold fluorescence.

In silence, he stared in awe. In his near view stood an enormous tree, whose branches of jeweled flora seemed to extend for a mile. Adding to the wonder, two more of those enormous angels materialized at his sides. Their form and presence were like the ones that welcomed them at the arch. Once again, he felt their ancient majesty and power. Yet he also saw them as confident gentle giants who radiated unconditional loving natures. Somehow, he knew they were guardians of the highest order.

As before, they did not speak, but just pointed him to the massive wonder of the tree while emitting light rays from the embossed symbols of the Alpha and Omega on their breastplates. The rays served to direct the way for Obe.

He took his first step in the direction of the palatial tree and wished that his friends were beside him in support as they had been before. He missed Tony most of all, and thought of how much he had frustrated him, but he had remained loyal and supportive of the older man.

Within a few steps, Obe realized that what he thought were flowers were, in actuality, Throne Angels. They were distinguishable by their form of wheels of fire, covered with eyes and wings that gave off a bright golden reflection, complementing the auras that wrapped them. They faced the tree, singing songs of praise to the majesty of God in a beautiful yet indistinguishable language. Their melodic sounds filled him with a deep sense of humility and uncontainable joy. Nevertheless, he felt anxious, knowing now that his time with God had come.

He attempted a delay by trying to release himself from the meditative state, but was unable to do so. His joy at being in the Presence was marred with apprehension.

Reality began to take hold. *This is it,* he moaned, knowing now that the long-due confrontation with God had arrived. He again tried to wake, reminding himself of their destination.

"Throne City," he muttered, and repeated, "Throne City." He tried to get a grip on what he thought was a change in plan, as if to delay the inevitable. "We were supposed to go to Throne City, all of us together."

A group of the miniature angelic creatures circled about his head, chattering with joy. One whispered words of consolation in his ear, "Be not afraid. You have entered the domain of ultimate Love and Mercy." After saying this, they merrily flew away into the mass of the countless throng of singing Throne angels.

Obe continued down the path to the base of the majestic tree that awaited him. Before it sat a simple marble pedestal, like that in Paraclete City. Instinctively, he knew to seat himself, and as he did, everything around him faded away.

In a moment, he was enveloped in a space of extreme light and energy, and a light that was more encompassing than anything he had experienced before.

The tree's colors glowed with greater intensity, and in an instant burst into flames. The air became heavy and filled with energy similar to that of the atmosphere when lightning strikes nearby. What followed was the profound utterance of a deep paternal voice.

So here you are, My dear child, son and brother of My Only begotten Son. There was a brief pause before the voice resumed in a deeper tone, *Why do you have not ears to listen? You say you love Me and marvel at the beauty and wonder of My creation. Your heart is full of love for My children, yet at the same time hardened so that you cannot see that of Mine. Nor the passionate love of my Son, the incarnation of man. His love surpasses all love. A love that defines infinite mercy. One that promises and fulfills; a trusted love.*

Obe trembled inside with mixed emotions—from fear, to joy, to wonderment. He was unable to speak, totally overwhelmed by God's hallowed voice.

So now, Obermyer Coddington, voice your disagreement.

Obe made three attempts to speak, trying to formulate non-inflammatory words.

God interjected, *What a man utters with conviction confirms the will of his heart. Stop skating around. Out with it.*

Obe stuttered out a fearful reply, "Almighty Master and Creator, You Who Are and Always Will Be, already know the tangles of my heart." He paused again to build courage. "Dear Heavenly Father, my heart has always been confounded with the thought that some souls would be damned to eternal Hell without possibility of reprieve or rehabilitation. Although they did unspeakable things, they did not ask to be born."

Obe squirmed in a spiritual sweat, expecting God's wrath.

The ground vibrated as the fiery bush erupted with plumes of fire. Obe, shaking in a panic, pre-empted God's reply.

"Almighty Father, through the graces and mercy You have shown me, especially here in the heavenly realm with my loving friends and mentors, I am beginning to understand the power and process of man's free will."

In a tone of controlled patience, God answered, *You're a piece of work, using the words of My child and your brother, Anthony Romero. But you're My piece of work, and I guess I have to take responsibility for that.* He bellowed with laughter, which both shocked and calmed Obe.

You apparently still know little about the depth of My love, grace, and mercy. And that of My Son, who suffered His sorrowful passion for the salvation of souls.

A stark silence seized the atmosphere. Nothing could be heard, no singing or utterance of any kind. Obe just sat, not knowing what to expect next.

He thought of Tony, and how he missed him and the others. In a dream-like vision, he found himself back aboard the boat, stepping into a holograph like the one of the St. Augustine lecture. Tony, Archangel Pinchot, Mason, and Cornelael were all beside him. They were at the precipice of a portal that opened into a tunnel of light, banded with coils of shimmering red energy that spiraled down to Earth.

Obe listened in as an undetected observer. Pinchot was about to speak, but Tony interrupted him. "I guess I'm going back, huh?"

"Only if you agree to."

"You mean I have a choice?"

"Of course you do. Remember, you have free will."

"Why? I mean, why am I being sent back?"

"God has chosen you to evangelize. To remove the bloodstain of mistrust and doubt from humanity, which is about to succumb to a darker fate."

Tony started to get excited about the prospect of seeing his wife and children again. "Norma? The kids?"

"Yes, you will be re-united with them."

"But I'm not a preacher or biblical scholar. I don't have the education and skills."

"You have God's love to take with you. Scripture is not a textbook or a legal document. When one digests it spiritually, and without judgment or prejudice, it is healing and life-giving. It is a book of love, one Divinely inspired. The Holy Spirit will provide you with the rest. Remember, everything is possible with God. And I will be by your side."

"After all this time, how can I go back? After all, they buried me."

"On the continuum, time is relative. However, *human* time may be running out. You will have the opportunity to work as God's instrument in rescuing souls from damnation."

"Me?"

"As your friend Mason is fond saying, *Let it unfold.*"

"Obe! What about Obe? Will he make it? Will I see him again?"

"I expect you will, and sooner than you think."

Obe, still listening, smiled with joy at the prospect of reuniting with Tony.

The holograph faded, and Obe was once more aware of the burning tree. He thought of Tony. *I knew he'd go back. He didn't feel worthy of being here. I'll miss him...if I remain here, that is.*

The misty golden light began to recede, and Obe found himself surrounded by a countless number of souls, all of whom were festooned in colorful tunics and singing their thanks and gratitude to him. He glanced over his shoulder, thinking that they were addressing another. But there wasn't anyone else in sight.

For a few moments, he bathed in the energy of their love, trying to understand their homage for him. He soon noticed the crowd parting, opening a path in their midst, and as they did, they transfigured into fluffy sparkling white sheep. Out from within them came Jesus, a portrait of complete perfection, radiating streams of red and white light from His heart. Atop His shoulders nestled a small lamb. Obe fell to his knees in awe.

Jesus stepped behind him and placed his hands on his shoulders, and Obe melted in extraordinary joy. "My Lord, My God, I am not worthy..."

Jesus interrupted, "Listen."

The sheep encircled about them as they changed back into human form. Obe listened to their grateful explanation. "Your prayers and heartfelt hope for our redemption helped us to gain relief of pain and ultimate release from the depths of Paraclete City. Included were many of our number who were bound for damnation." They told him how they were able to repent, and to learn to love God and themselves through the example of Obe's suffering for them.

Obe cried with joy, giving thanks to Jesus from the center of his soul. At last, part of his dream had been realized.

And in an instant, they were gone, leaving Obe with Jesus by his side, and engulfed in raw energy as their eyes fixed on the burning tree.

Once again, God spoke out in a thunderous voice, *He calls Us to a challenge, My beloved Son and Redeemer of Humanity. Our hearts are already heavily laden on what We must do.*

Silence reigned for what seemed to Obe to be a millennia before words were spoken again.

The burning tree exploded once again with God's thunderous voice, now mixed with both annoyance and sadness. *It is time for the last sign. The final battle for souls is now imminent. The bloodstain of your Passion and sadness is soon to be adjudicated, My Son.*

Jesus gripped both of Obe's arms and looked deeply into his eyes. "Will you herald Me, as your prophetic forefathers did? When you have eyes to see?"

"I will. I will, my Great Lord," Obe answered contritely.

The voices of the singing angels became louder. Then Jesus melded into the fiery tree, and a white dove descended over Obe's head as he fell into a dreamlike state once again.

This time he found himself with Riccardo, who held his hand and led him to a portal. Obe heard his own words as he drifted into a deeper state of transition.

"Me? I'm going back too?"

Thirty-two

Forlorn, Norma Romero and Tony's mother dangled rosary beads from their hands while they waited on a dimly-lit train platform at Grand Central. Beside them, Tony's father swallowed hard. He held tightly onto the hands of his grandchildren, Cookie and Anthony Jr. Cookie whimpered, clutching her teddy bear to her chest, as she looked down the tracks for her train home.

Pinchot appeared in his white tuxedo on a nearby platform bench, and beckoned Cookie with a wave of his hand. The child broke her grandfather's grip and pointed to the bench. Grandpa wasn't paying attention, so with her teddy bear in tow she joined Pinchot on the bench.

Unseen by the others, Pinchot imparted a warm smile to her, "Sweet precious child of God, do not weep. Your father lives. Tell your mother to return to the hospital."

As the train pulled into the station with the loud squeal of brakes, Cookie bolted for her mom.

"Mommy! Mommy!" she shouted, "We have to go back! Daddy is alive!"

Norma stooped down to comfort her. "Honey, we have to go home now." She looked up in silence at her mother-in-law, who simply shook her head sadly.

The train came to a stop, the doors opened, and passengers got off. Just as Norma and her family were about to enter, Cookie broke her grip and ran toward the stairwell. Norma raced to retrieve her.

Cookie called out once more as she started to climb the stairs, "Mommy... Daddy is alive! The man in the white suit told me. We have to go to the hospital!"

The train pulled out, leaving them behind in a cloud of track debris. Norma took Cookie's hand as the youngster was about to mount the fourth step.

"A man in a white suit?"

"Yes!" She appealed with sad eyes to her mother and grandparents behind her. "We have to go!"

"Okay, honey we'll go back," Norma assured her. She turned and whispered to her in-laws, "We might just as well, since we missed the train. I'll call the nurse and ask her to help with Cookie."

They climbed the set of grimy stairs now crowded with commuters. The stairwell took on the scent of burnt diesel. They gratefully took a breath of fresh air when they reached the main level of the station. Norma headed for a nearby phone booth, searching for change in her purse. Tony's father stopped her; he had already dug some out and handed the coins to her. She patted his cheek and wiped tears from his face as she placed the coins in the slot and dialed the nurse's station--a number tattooed into her memory.

Norma looked at her children with sadness as she waited for her call to be answered.

"ICU... Carmichael."

Norma took a deep breath. "Hi Nurse Carmichael, Norma Romero. We have a situ..."

Carmichael spoke over her, "Oh, Mrs. Romero! Great! I just left a message for you. Where are you?"

Norma blinked in surprise. "We are still at Grand Central," she said.

"Doctor wants you to come back right-away... Mrs. ..."

Norma dropped the phone, and in a shot took her children in tow toward the taxi stand, with their bewildered grandparents trailing behind.

The undertaker exited the elevator, rolling Tony's remains in a body bag on a gurney toward the back exit of Beekman's security desk. He handed the security guard the release papers and made idle conversation. As he did, Pinchot materialized in his white suit.

"Your patient moved," he advised, pointing to the gurney.

The undertaker and the security guard looked up at him, thinking him strange.

"Oh, that's not unusual. Reflexes," the undertaker answered, with a smile on his face and a glance to the security guard. Then he heard an unmistakable sound--a groan. When he looked at the body bag, he saw movement, and quickly zipped it open. He froze for a moment when he saw Tony's chest laboring a breath.

"Jesus, Mary and Joseph! He's alive!" he shouted.

"Exactly. Praise them," Pinchot affirmed. He disappeared in the confusion of people who began to gather, while the security guard nervously called in a code blue.

Norma paced in the ICU waiting room, as Tony's parents and her children sat with anticipation. In what seemed to them hours, although it was only minutes, the doctor came in with an astounded look upon his face. Without a moment's hesitation, he blurted out, "Mrs. Romero, your husband is alive..."

All came to their feet and rushed to him. Cookie and Anthony Jr. hugged Norma, who became faint. The doctor reached out to steady her as Cookie screamed with joy. "I told you... I told you, Mommy! The man said it!"

"He was about to be placed in the hearse. A bona fide miracle. His life signs are strong, and he appears to be coming out of the coma. God's hand in it for sure," the doctor said, with a disbelieving shake of his head.

Later that evening Tony, still unconscious, seemed to be comfortable as he lay in his hospital bed hooked up to machines and intravenous. Anthony Jr. and Cookie played a card game while Norma, wrapped in a blanket, slept in a chair.

Cookie saw her father move and ran to his side, and Anthony Jr. followed suit. Tony's eyes flickered and opened, and Cookie shouted, "Daddy! Daddy! Anthony, wake up Mommy!"

Little Anthony shook Norma. "Mommy! Daddy... waked up..."

Norma opened her eyes and bolted off the chair to join her children at bedside. She called his name, and Tony's eyes opened. He looked at her and began to move his lips, trying to form a word. Norma, teary-eyed, gripped his hand and calmed her excited children with a hand movement. She spoke to him in a gentle voice, "Tony, can you hear me? It's Norma..."

"Yes," he answered faintly, "I hear you. Where am I?"

Norma shouted with excitement, "Cookie, call the nurse! And get grandma and grandpa from the waiting room!"

She leaned in to her husband. "Tony you're in the hospital." Then, with a breath of relief, she added, "Oh God! Tony, you've been in a coma for over a week, and literally on the way to the undertaker." Norma closed her eyes and mouthed a prayerful *thank you.* "How do you feel?"

Tony answered her in a strained voice, "I have a headache. Where's Pinchot... Obe?" "Obe? Pinchot? Who are they?" Norma questioned.

Tony took a moment to respond. "I guess it was a dream after all."

Doctors and nurses scurried into the room, and ushered Norma aside to examine Tony. Patients and staff, hearing a commotion, peered in through the glass partition.

Carmichael, the Head Nurse, held Norma, with joyful tears cascading down her cheeks. "A miracle, a true miracle! Blessed be God!" she cheered.

Thirty-three

NORMA SLID THE BLINDS OPEN in her bedroom. Tony, lying in bed, gazed up at the ceiling. Norma went over to him, a paper bag in her hand.

"Tony, you have been lying in bed for a week. The doctors think that you should be up and about," she encouraged.

"I just don't feel up to it," he answered groggily.

"The doctor said that it wasn't unusual to be depressed after coming out of a coma. He said it's important to exercise."

"Norma, I don't feel as if I belong here. The dream I had about another place lingers in my head. It's as if I want to go back," he said, as he continued to stare at the ceiling. Then he said under his breath, "Linger?"

"What?" she questioned. She waited for an answer but received none.

Tony sat up and saw the paper bag on the nightstand. "What's that?"

"That's the stuff you had at the hospital. I'll go down and make breakfast. Try to come down. I think you need a shower too."

Tony turned over, reluctant to rise and take a shower. After a moment he pushed himself and sat up. *I got to do this for Norma,* he said to himself.

After he showered and struggled to put on his robe, he wobbled to the bed, wincing with muscle cramps. He sat on its edge, and noticed again the paper bag on the nightstand.

He reached for it and spilled out its contents on the bed. A sun streak cracked through the window blinds and illuminated a gold watch in its midst. Tony caught the reflection and picked it up.

When he saw that its face had no dials, he jumped up with joy and shouted, "Norma! Norma, it's true...it's all true... Praise God!"

Within seconds, Norma rushed into the room, potholder and spatula in hand. With a worried look and tone, she asked, "Are you okay?"

Tony, shaking with joy, wrapped his arms around her and lifted her off the floor in a bear hug. "I'm okay! No, a better word would be 'fantastic'!"

Norma panicked and squirmed out of his grasp. "Sit down," she ordered. "Maybe this is too soon. You need to adjust."

Pinchot, in his white tuxedo, and Obe, in a dazzling white tunic all aglow, materialized and motioned to Tony to slow down. Tony, with a euphoric expression on his face, started toward them with outstretched arms.

"Pinchot! Obe!" he called.

Norma held him in her arms to calm him. "Let's get you dressed and some food into you. Maybe some fresh air will help."

She shook her head and dashed to the dresser for clothes, mumbling to herself, "Oh God... imaginary friends. I guess the doctors left that out."

After dressing, Tony came down to the kitchen to find Norma at the counter making waffles. He took a bite of a waffle, then wrapped his arms around her.

"Waffles! Fantastic!" He laughed and cried out, "Thank you, Cornelael!"

Norma grabbed him and stared hard into his eyes. She expected to find madness, but instead she cried in surprise, "Your eyes are sparkling, and you're all aglow!"

Befuddled, she demanded, "What's going on here?" Then she mumbled to herself, trying to understand, "Cornelael?" Inside, she was experiencing turmoil, fearing for her husband's sanity

Oh my God, another imaginary friend, Tony?

Tony squeezed her once more and kissed her on the temple. "Norma, my love, I have a lot to tell you. Glorious things."

A ring of the doorbell interrupted him. Norma patted his face and made for the door with Tony right behind her.

She opened it, and standing there with bouquets of flowers and boxes of candy were Cynthia and Arthur Raymon with their daughter Gloria, along with Joe Barone and Jimmy Murphy. A reporter and cameraman lurked behind them, with a TV-News truck in the background.

To their astonishment, Tony warmly hugged each of them with joy, and lifted little Gloria into his arms as he invited them in. He also hugged the news crew as they filmed, which caused the camera to go off-kilter.

The reporter questioned Tony, "Mr. Romero, do you know that the public calls you 'Miracle Man'?"

Tony smiled, "Me? The only miracle man is God."

He gestured to the child in his arms. "See a true miracle of creation. The beauty of life." He winked at little Gloria. "I have a lot to share, but please forgive me for now. I wish some time alone with my friends." He waved to the camera. "Blessings to all."

Tony entered the living room to join the others.

"Norma, we're going to need more waffles." He kissed Gloria, still in his arms, and laughed. "Ice cream too." He sat and looked over at a picture of Jesus hanging on the wall. He glanced upward and prayed, *There's a lot to do Lord,* and bowed his head.

Thirty-four

THREE WEEKS PASSED. Tony's life was now filled with constant interviews. Meetings with journalists, clergy, and religious groups from every denomination filled his daily calendar. Tony was on a roll, compelled by a sense of urgency to tell his story to all who would hear it. His earthly quest now was to reach as many souls as he could, to encourage humanity to turn to God.

An investigative reporter, looking to dispel Tony's account of having a celestial encounter with a teenage colonial, challenged him in a most unusual way. He requested that the Fayetteville Police Department unearth Obe Coddington's remains, which Tony alleged lay buried next to a boulder in the backyard of a suburban home--the place that Tony claimed he had visited with the spirit of Obe.

Accepting the challenge, it did not take long for Fayetteville's finest to locate the home. The boulder was a well-known landmark in the community due to its enormous size.

Within a week's time, Tony and Norma found themselves, with invisible Archangel Pinchot and Obe at their sides, on a bright shiny southern day under the suspicious eyes of Fayetteville's Mayor and Police Chief. Also present were reporters and a crowd of neighbors, who watched the men dig for Obe's remains. The police chief eyed Tony with skepticism. He thought this whole exercise was the folly of a northern, big city weirdo.

It did not take long before they heard a digger shout from the shallow pit.

"I think I've got something! Looks like a skull," he said, then added, "Yes, bones too."

The spectators gasped, Norma included.

The police chief gripped Tony's arm. "Mr. Romero, this is now an open investigation. I'll need your complete statement at the station, and you'll need to turn over your passport."

Tony nodded with a knowing smile. Under his breath he spoke to Obe by his side, "Okay, buddy, now you'll have a proper burial.'

Hearing him, Norma shot him a look, and admonished him under her breath, "You've got to be kidding."

Norma's attitude changed to fear as the news reporters encircled Tony, firing questions. Pinchot placed a hand on her shoulder, and she calmed, although she couldn't say why.

She did not know what to believe. Was what he was saying true? Had he visited heaven? She was hopeful that Tony's doctors would shed light on his behavior at his next appointment. She needed help.

Tony sat on an examination table, buttoning his shirt and waiting to hear the doctor's assessments of the test results. Norma sat next to him, hoping for the doctor to make sense of it all for her.

The doctor completed his examination notes with a confused look on his face, and turned to Tony. Norma tensed, but Tony just smiled.

"Tony, you're as sound as a prize fighter about to enter the ring. What baffles me and the other doctors is that large red stain on your chest. It's not a rash or viral in nature, nor is it a birthmark. It appears to be an insoluble stain of blood."

Tony took the doctor's hand and placed it on the mark. "Doctor, trust me. Close your eyes, clear your mind, and feel the passion of Our Lord."

Humoring him, the Doctor closed his eyes. In a second, he was filled with sadness, then joy, and then he became giddy.

Norma rolled her eyes, shook her head in annoyance, and interrupted. "Time to go, Tony. Thank you, Doctor."

Without regard to what the doctor was experiencing, she rose in a shot and ushered Tony out to their car.

Norma started the car and looked at him.

"We gotta talk," she told him with a shake to her voice. "I called Father Sparachino, and he's coming over later."

"Father Sparachino? That's great! He gave me a wonderful send-off."

Norma rolled her eyes as they pulled away.

Later that evening, Norma and Tony visited with Father Sparachino in their living room. Norma had prepared a pot of espresso and a tray of Italian cookies. After the priest had bitten into one of the biscotti and had taken a couple of sips of coffee, Tony gave him a rundown of what he had experienced. Norma listened with an objective ear for the first time since Tony had come home from the hospital.

The priest grew pale and stared in shock at him, his lip quivering.

Norma noticed the effect Tony's words had on the old priest.

"Father, are you okay?"

"Yes, Norma," he said, somewhat distractedly. "I'm just trying to sort all this out in my mind. I think I should pray some. If you don't mind, I would like to take a walk."

He got up. "I'll be right back to hear more." He sped to the front door as if he had just had an attack of claustrophobia.

Norma placed her hand on her temple and shook her head. "Tony, you rocked that poor old man."

"Have faith, Norma. The Holy Spirit will inform him. He is a man of strong faith and love for the Lord."

Norma spat back, "Will He inform me too? I'm confused as hell, Tony."

"Yes, He will. I'm sorry, my love, but we all have our own work to do for the glory of God."

Norma slapped him, and followed up with a bite of repressed fury, "You leave the house as a philanderer, get hit by a truck, go into a coma, and come out of it a prophet?"

Norma forced herself to calm down. She rubbed his face and lowered her voice. "Sorry, but don't you think this is all a little hard to digest?"

Tony saw that Pinchot and Obe were there in support. "Oh yes, I know. Believe me, I know."

He gripped her as if she were a precious treasure. "The Lord is calling us to rise above ourselves. To help Him shepherd His children, because time is growing short for humanity. All of heaven is in an uproar."

Norma broke the embrace and began to cry. Tony tried to hug her once more but she pushed him away.

"Norma, I deserve more than a slap on the face. What I did to you and our children was unconscionable. Please forgive me. I'm not the same man I was before."

Thirty-five

NORMA AND FATHER SPARACHINO were jittery as they entered the TV station building. Following behind were the invisible spirits of Obe and Archangel Pinchot. Tony pointed them to the billboard and explained to his invisible companions, "The 'Talk of Talk Shows' is one of New York's biggest, and has a national and international audience. A good forum to get the message out."

The talk show host, along with Tony, Norma, and Father Sparachino, were joined by Rabbi Golden, a Jewish theologian, and Papal Nuncio Father Riccardo Gutierrez. They all sat on armchairs prepared in a semi-circle on the set. The audience applauded as the talk show host greeted them.

"Thank you. We have an interesting topic to discuss tonight," he said. "Let me introduce our panel. First, Anthony Romero. I guess you could call him a visionary. That okay Tony?"

Tony gave him a humble smile and a nod.

"And Mrs. Romero, along with Spiritual Director Father Frank Sparachino. We also have Rabbi Moshe Golden,

President of the National Council of Conservative Rabbis, and Father Riccardo Gutierrez, Church Apologist." All smiled and waved to the audience in acknowledgement.

The host pointed to a large TV Monitor on stage. "First, I would like to show a video clip of the exhumation of the remains of Obermyer Coddington, a nineteenth-century farm boy. This operation was conducted by the Mayor and Police Chief of Fayetteville, North Carolina, who were also asked to join the panel but declined. In the video montage, you will see and hear the unearthing process of Mr. Coddington's remains, a boy who Mr. Romero alleges to be his spirit friend, alive and well in Heaven. And sometimes here on earth. Right Tony?

Tony nodded and looked over his shoulder with a smile.

"We will also see an interview with a research scientist, who also declined to join our panel. Later, we will take you to the burial site of Mr. Coddington's mother and sister in Georgia, the location of which was their farm at that time. The strip will also include a reporter's interview with the Romero family undertaker and Tony's doctors. We'll end with a metallurgist's evaluation of the...unique, to say the least...gold watch that Mr. Romero claims is a celestial gift. Then we will come back here for our panel discussion."

The producers ran the film, and the audience was mesmerized by what they saw and felt. They sat in dead silence when the video clip ended. A flashing applause sign broke their silence, and they clapped their hands in response.

The talk show host, who also seemed to be in a daze of wonderment himself, directed his first question to Tony. "Mr. Romero, this all seems hard to dispute. Especially your ability to locate Mr. Coddington's remains."

"Everything is possible with God," Tony answered him.

Rabbi Golden raised his hand. "Mr. Romero, why do you think God made this possible? And for that matter, why did He select you?"

"Why He selected me is a mystery. I wasn't a very nice person." Tony paused for breath. "I guess I can be an example of redemption."

Tony glanced at Norma and continued, "Why He made this possible is because, I believe, that time is growing short for humanity. There have been many apparitions of the Blessed Virgin Mary over the years. They continue today, whereby she calls the world to faith and trust in God. But not many appear to be listening to her advice. I was one of those with deaf ears myself.

"We can't use reason to find God. All that's required is an open heart to see Him and hear Him in everything and everyone. When we read Scripture, we need to feel the words, for they live and breathe Him. As we do when we hear a child speak, it should be that we don't just listen to their words--we feel the love inside them and us.

"God wants all of His children to share in eternal life with Him. But to do so we must believe, and trust in Him, and follow His will."

Father Gutierrez interjected, "Mr. Romero, tell me. After experiencing Heaven, were you able to learn what the true religion is?"

Tony laughed before he answered. "Oh, Father. God didn't make all these religions, we did. Our God-given free will is a powerful gift. Unfortunately for some, a curse. God does not mess with that. It's our choice. He sends graces to exercise it for the good, but in the end it is our choice."

The host remarked, doubt in his voice, "It must have been hard for you to return here after experiencing the wonders of Heaven that you described."

Tony smiled and replied, "It's been quite an adjustment. Feeling physical pain and emotional strife once more." Then he turned to the audience. His eyes seemed to penetrate each one.

"Although I am grateful to God for the opportunity to show, to both my family and the world, the love I should have shown in the past, I am also grateful to suffer for those that do not know Him--those in jeopardy."

The host now probed Norma. "Mrs. Romero, how did you adjust to all this?"

"'Adjust'. That's a mild way of putting it." Norma paused to give Tony an endearing pat on his leg. "At first, like so many others, I thought that the coma had affected him. However, the enormous amount of love that has flowed from him has overwhelmed me. He now has a resilient peace and kindness about him. I guess I can call it a peaceful resolve."

"Sorry, but I must ask. Do you believe all this?" the host zipped back.

Norma unbuttoned her blouse to show a red blotch on her chest. The audience gasped. Father Sparachino stood to undo his collar and unbutton his shirt, also to show a red blotch. The audience gasped again.

The priest shared, "I guess I got knocked on the head too. One morning, as I was about to shave, I saw the blotch in the mirror. I fell to my knees in prayers of thanksgiving for this special gift, to share in the Lord's Passion."

The host's face paled, and he fumbled out another question. "Mr.... Mr... Ro...mero. What do you believe God is asking ...us to do?"

"Easy," he said. "Just turn to Him...love Him and help your fellow man find Him too. So none are lost. Emulate Obe's self-sacrificing hope for humanity."

Tony's eyes searched upward. "The blotches represent Our Lord's sorrowful Passion." He looked over his shoulder at Obe.

"Why did you look over your shoulder? See something?" the host asked in an incredulous tone. Tony peeked back again to Obe and Pinchot, invisible to the others, who rested their hands on him.

Not waiting for a reply the host shot out another question.

"Mr. Romero, many people have claimed to see a golden light shadowing you."

Tony interrupted and pointed to the host's side. The host followed his eyes.

Obe, in a golden mist, stood next to him with a smile. "Oh, yes, that's Obe. In fact, he's standing right next to you. Ready to open your heart."

The host cracked a grin and reached out next to himself in comic disbelief. The audience laughed.

The laughter soon changed into shock. Obe took the man's hand, and the man began to glow. He immediately came to his feet, and shouted to the audience in a state of euphoria, "It is true, it's all true! We must turn to God!

The audience laughed and laughed until they realized he was serious. That he was not joking.

Tony rose to embrace him and just said, "Amen."

ACKNOWLEDGEMENTS

I would like to express my deep gratitude to my many friends for test reading this work, motivating me and providing me with constructive suggestions, criticisms, and prayers.

Special mention must be made of my wife *Consuelo* and my dear friends Leila and Don Kazimir, for their motivation, critique and advice in the writing process, also to Michael Herzog C.G.I. Artist/Illustrator for the Cover Image and Typesetting and Rev. Kevin C. Nelson, who generously helped in the editing process. And, Tracy Atkins of Bookdesigner.com for his help in the production process. And, my childhood friend Carmine Crudele for his support and help in the editing process.

And, last but not least, my deepest expression to my editor: Author, KATHY REE, for making the production of the book possible.

ABOUT THE AUTHOR

The author's first writing project was a non-fiction book about the Apparitions of the Blessed Virgin Mary in the small village of Medjugorje in then Yugoslavia, now Bosnia-Herzegovina. Titled: "Medjugorje, A Pilgrim's Journey." Originally published in 1991; with the forward and collaboration by Author, John Westermann (Exit Wounds). Because of popular demand it was re-released (Second Edition) in 2010. Also, the book is in the process of its Spanish language translation due for completion-2015.

He recently published; "The Hester Street Kids" a Drama/Thriller and his first work of fiction provides an historical view of the 1950's era and of the power of the Sicilian Mob in New York at that time. A saga, one that talks to the plight of Italian American immigrants striving for a living in the new world under the thumbs of the Sicilian Mafia.

Armando has also written the screenplay adaptions for both "SCHISM" and "THE HESTER STREET KIDS."

He was awarded a Bachelor of Science Social Welfare with a minor in psychology and a Master's of Science in Clinical Social Work from Fordham University Graduate School of Social Service with emphasis on psycho-dynamic psychotherapy.

PRAYERS FOR SOULS IN PURGATORY

Eternal Father, I offer Thee the Most Precious Blood of Thy Divine Son, Jesus, in union with the Masses said throughout the world today, for all the holy souls in purgatory, for sinners everywhere, for sinners in the universal church, those in my own home and within my family.

Amen.

The Prayer of St. Gertrude, above, is one of the most famous of the prayers for souls in purgatory. St. Gertrude the Great was a Benedictine nun and mystic who lived in the 13th century. According to tradition, our Lord promised her that 1000 souls would be released from purgatory each time it is said devoutly

www.ingramcontent.com/pod-product-compliance
Lightning Source LLC
Chambersburg PA
CBHW030811310726
48980CB00006B/466/J

* 9 7 8 0 9 6 3 0 5 4 4 8 7 *